1

MORE

PRIDEAUX

GHOST STORIES

FEATURING THE PRIDEAUXS

OF BIGBURY, RINGMORE AND

CHUDLEIGH

4

A CIP catalogue record for this title is

available from the British Library.

ISBN 978-0-9954609-3-5

www.paganuspublishing.co.uk

First Published in 2016

Paganus Publishing

Ruthin

Denbighshire

Paganus Publishing

FOREWORD

More Prideaux Ghost Stories is the latest in the series of Prideaux Ghost Stories. Chronologically the stories follow those in the book **Prideaux Ghost Stories** and **A Ghost Story** and preceding **Further Prideaux Ghost Stories.**

Each story features a generation of the family in my line. The people, houses, villages and timelines are correct in each story. Some features of the stories have either been passed down or added by the author with a great deal of poetic licence.

The Bigbury Butcher features Peter Prideaux. This is a tale of mysterious deaths and cruel betrayals in 17th Devon. Will there be any justice?

The Ringmore Wraiths features Peter Prideaux, son of the above. This is a story about a terrible beginning in life and how a call for help to beyond the grave can make a real difference. An unusual painting and magic spells conjure release from a lofty prison.

The Lanlivery Lights features Peter Prideaux, son and grandson of the above. This story involves underage sex resulting in a trip back to Cornwall where a decades old mining mystery is solved.

The Chudleigh Charity features Thomas Peter Prideaux, the son, grandson and great grandson of the above. This is a story of an unpopular wedding and control of a town by devious means. The otherworldly guardians of secret documents don't want to let go.

CAST LIST

As with the other Prideaux Ghost Stories books, names are repeated regularly and I find it helpful to differentiate between the Prideauxs in order to lessen irritation and the constant cry from the reader of, 'which Prideaux is she talking about now?'

Remember that these characters not only existed but are ancestors of mine.

The Bigbury Butcher - Peter Prideaux (1651-1725)
Born on the 22nd October 1651 and married;
Elizabeth Saunders on the 27th July 1684 at Aveton Gifford and she died 13th April 1686
Jane Boon on the 26th June 1687 in Bigbury
Joan Stone on the 28th May 1689 in Bigbury
Anne Baron in 1694 in Bigbury and died in 1701
8Peter and Anne had Peter in 1695, Ann in 1697 and Mary in 1701. Both Ann and Mary died in 1701.

The Ringmore Wraiths – Peter Prideaux (1695– 14th April 1749)
Married Joan who died on the 3rd August 1756
Their children were;
Joan born 30th September 1728
Elizabeth born 30th March 1732
Peter born 1st August 1733

Anne born 7th June 1736
Thomas born 17th December 1738

The Lanlivery Lights –Peter Prideaux (1st August 1733 - 1810)
Married Mary Wills on 10th May 1769
Their children were;
Thomas Peter born 26th December 1768
Peter born 14th November 1770
Jenny born 31st December 1775
John born 23rd March 1779

The Chudleigh Charity – Thomas Peter (26th December 1768 – 10th January 1842)
Married Charity Strong (2nd January 1770 13t November 1832) on the 13th November 1792
Their children were;
Thomas born 11th May 1793
John born 23rd March 1796
Ann born 4th November 1798
William born 8th June 1801
Peter born 30th January 1805
Mary born 24th December 1809
James born June 1881 and died August 1811

CONTENTS

THE BIGBURY BUTCHER
featuring Peter Prideaux 1651 – 1725

"To murder one wife is sin enough, but four wives is the work of a madman."

This statement was presented to me by the magistrate and I do not feel like answering him. What a stupid thing to say to me. I don't care about sin and I am certainly not mad. Indeed a true madman would not be able to consider whether or not he was mad. I am considering it and coming to the rapid conclusion that I am not mad.

"I see." I decide to give the answer the magistrate seems to want. The answer however does not satisfy him and he grimaces and looks back at the papers on the table in front of him.

We are not in court, just at the Modbury home of Sir William Bigbury. He does not know that I know that he knows that one of my ancestors killed one of his.

Sir William would call it murder if asked, whereas our family called it a duel. And this duel was caused by the Bigburys and their appalling behaviour. This bad blood had been going on between the families for centuries and Sir William enjoyed seeing Peter Prideaux across the table from him under questioning. He wasn't acknowledging that my Grandmother Blanche was an aunt or a cousin of his. I don't know which it is for we never spent any Christmases together. But I do know that the ghost of an ancestor of theirs and therefore mine burnt down their Hall in Cornwood. I decided not to bring it up here.

"Mr Baron, your father in law has advised me that your wife was killed by you using the same method it is generally believed you killed your previous three wives. He says that he has the evidence in the form of a letter from his daughter. There is also a similar accusation concerning the death of your two daughters."

"What method is that then?" I ask him.

This interview was becoming more surreal.

"We shall come to that later Mr Prideaux," he answers without looking up from his papers.

I expect that this way of dealing with me makes Sir William feel very important. Two can play at that game because I feel that I am quite important too.

"You don't have any right to keep me here, Sir William. There is no proof about any murder."

"What makes you so sure about that?"

"Because there were no murders," I say simply.

I have to stand – stand mark you – while these idiots fiddle about with papers and books for another ten minutes or so. Every so often there is a surly glance in my direction from Sir William and finally I announce,

"I am leaving now Bigbury. You have nothing on me and I have done nothing wrong. If you wish to speak to me about this again, then please deal with my solicitor at Modbury."

I walk out of the room and no one tries to stop me. A maid rushes towards me and hands me my hat and cane. Stupid girls always want an excuse to be near to me. I reward her with my best smile and she blushes and bobs a curtsey. She watches as I leave and untie my horse. I mount and ride away from the home of Sir William while pondering the interview which had just taken place.

As I glance back at the house, I notice a group of women standing on the stone steps. There are two children playing on the ground in front of them. I nod and the women place bony fingers upon their own lips, so I ride away swiftly.

Creepy servants Bigbury insists on employing.

I wave to one of my neighbours as I ride through the gate and trot back to the village. He does not wave back and I wonder why that should be. I kick my horse on and am soon outside my own property.

Although my house is larger than many in the village, most being cottages, it is still mortgaged via the Bigbury estate and I expect that this could now start to become a problem.

Walking in through the front door, I am met by my housekeeper, Mrs Thomas.

"Where is Peter?" I ask her.

"He is upstairs with that housekeeper woman, Miss Gardener," she answers.

Mrs Thomas does not approve of the pretty young woman who was employed by me after the death of my last wife. I personally could not care less about what Mrs Thomas thinks. She is employed as a cook and not my adviser.

"Bring me some food and I shall eat in the dining room. Go and ask Miss Gardener to come down and see me there now. I do not want to see the boy, just her."

That should give her plenty to think about - nosy old woman.

I wander into the dining room and sit at the table. Every so often in comes Mrs Thomas to set the table or bring in food and drink, but eventually in walks the delectable Miss Gardener.

"Sit down Miss Gardener," I tell her.

It is nice watching a young woman in my employ doing as she is told while refusing to look me in the eye. This is a more powerful feeling than marrying a young girl knowing that she would give in to me quickly and without question. I suppose that is because I am very good looking and charming when I want to be and all my little brides believed I was in love with them. It was too easy.

"Have you heard about my meeting with Sir William this morning?"

"I know you went there Sir, but I don't know why," she answers.

"You have not been listening to the talk then."

Her eyes were still downcast while she ate her soup and so gave nothing away to me. I know she is lying though. Everyone has heard the gossip even if they have not taken any part in it.

"No Sir."

We continue, eating in silence, she avoiding the touch of my hand when I reach for the bread at the same time as her. When I laugh at this, she blushes crimson. After the meal, I tell her to go back upstairs and look after the boy. She does so without question - of course.

I walk into the library in order to smoke and to think.

I met Elizabeth Saunders in Bigbury, where I moved almost immediately after I received my inheritance. . Elizabeth was quite a pretty girl and the daughter and heir of a gentleman, William Saunders from Aveton Gifford. Her mother and brother had died of a fever within two days of each other in 1681 - her mother Elizabeth on the 3rd and her brother and co heir Thomas on the 5th February. As Father and my brother James had died only a few months prior to her loss, we had a good deal in common.

My father and James died so close in time to each other, of poisoning the doctor said. And it is a terrible responsibility when your mother dies bringing you into the world. There is so much to prove, you see. I have to make my life count and therefore Mother's death need not be in vain.

Elizabeth's family on hearing that I had received a substantial inheritance opened their house and ultimately, their niece and her inheritance to me.

Aveton Gifford is a pretty village sitting at the head of the estuary and has a lovely church and bridge. I used to travel there by horse from Bigbury, through St Ann's Chapel and down a steep track to the tidal road which runs along the estuary. This road would be covered by the sea when the tide is high. It is a very pleasant drive and one which I have taken many times during my life.

At the dinner I attended when the Saunders family was first introduced to me, I decided that I must work fast on this girl in order to win her and her dowry. Being a sociable fellow, I had already wooed many local girls and the richer ones had been kept well away from me by their wary fathers. Being the great nephew of a Bishop and the grandson of a farmer of a large estate held little sway now that the Prideauxs had lost a good deal of ground and standing during Cromwell's time. It really was not right and I intended to live the life I should have been entitled to. When my father recently died, the money left to me and my brother was enough to set me on the right track again. And as my sights are set very high, I intend to use my considerable charms on the ladies with money and marry one of them. It seems fair enough to me.

I married Elizabeth Saunders on the 27th July 1684 in Aveton Gifford church at a ceremony attended by her family and my brother Andrew. The wedding was a great success which it had to be considering how much Elizabeth's father; William Saunders had spent on the event. He seemed to invite most of the village and in all it was a very gay affair. I have to say I enjoyed myself.

When we returned to our house for our wedding night at our new property in Aveton Gifford, courtesy of Saunders, I found Elizabeth to be totally inexperienced and shy. This was a good omen and I think that I made the whole event a pleasant one for my new bride - I enjoyed myself anyway.

We waited for the news of a pregnancy and were disappointed. I continued to be disappointed every month and spent a good deal of my time ensuring that I was giving all the correct attention was given to Elizabeth in order for a pregnancy to occur. I wanted a son, no daughters, just a son, or two. When I was not paying attention to my lovely wife I enjoyed the races, hunting and drinking and a lot of gambling. I was never as lucky with gambling as I should have been and money seemed to leave me much more easily than it ever arrived. Elizabeth felt that I was spending too much money on these pastimes and I told her that it was none of her business. All the money in our marriage was mine and no arguments.

She spent her days organising the house and gardens. She was very good at doing that and I allowed her to help out at the church sometimes. She was just absolutely useless at producing children and I was beginning to hope that I had not married a barren cow.

When the second Christmas of our union had passed with no blessing, I worried that I was never going to be a father. Elizabeth said that I was putting too much pressure on her, but I disagreed. She was young and perfectly capable of producing a son if she put her mind to it.

We spent Christmas with my Stowford family and I became angered by the constant referrals to our lack of issue. This was not seemly, so something would have to be done - there was no getting away from that.

With there being no baby by the time Easter arrived, I decided that a change of diet was called for and insisted that I supervised the preparation of my wife's food from now on.

Unfortunately poor Elizabeth died of food poisoning in April and we buried her on the 13th April 1687.

I was desolate naturally and could take comfort from no one, although I have to say that her family were less than sympathetic to my loss. As soon as Elizabeth's estate was finalised the large house in which we had been living at the time of her demise came to me entirely as her husband along with certain sums of money and so after a while, I was content.

Along came little Jane Boon. Now she was a precious young girl, as fair as Elizabeth had been dark and equally as pretty. I noticed Jane at the party which was attended by many of my friends at Bigbury towards Christmas the previous year. Elizabeth had been too sickly to attend. Jane was sweet and innocent and looked down at her pretty feet when I smiled at her. At 36 years old I still had good looks and the bearing of a gentleman and it was relatively easy to catch the eye of a shy and as luck would have it, rich young lady.

After discussing the matter with her parents and promising to sell my house in Aveton Gifford and move to Bigbury in order that their beloved daughter could be seen by her mother every day, a marriage was arranged for the 26th June 1687.

I bought a lovely house just outside the village, hired the servants recommended by my mother-in-law-to-be and set up home. The Boons were very happy with the match and settled a good sum on their daughter which I would of course be able to take charge of. They had no worries about this as I was quite evidently a rich man.

The wedding surpassed my first. Jane was not to be denied her day just because I was a widower and she my second wife. There were many guests and lots of food and flowers and the villagers turned out to wave and clap. What a day! I even noticed that one of my ancestors, Ralph Prideaux had once been Rector at the church.

Jane had promised me many children as she understood my disappointments to date. She said that she would say special prayers for a son to arrive nine months after our wedding. I performed my duty again and again. Jane did not always seem very receptive and told me that I was frightening her. I of course told her not to be so silly and carried on with my God given duty. She cried the first time and the second and the third. Girls are so manipulative with the little games they play. I don't think I shall ever understand them.

Her prayers came to nothing however. I asked her every month if we were to expect a son and she denied me each time. Really, this was too much.

Jane kept telling me that she was unwell and I did notice that's she was beginning to look pale and sad in a manner reminiscent of my dear Elizabeth. I told Jane so and reminded her that Elizabeth had eventually taken her dark depressions to the grave.

Jane spent a good deal of time visiting her mother or having her mother visit us, until I insisted that she cease. I told her mother that the visits were tiring Jane. I began supervising her food, adding herbs here and there which I told her would make her feel much better. I wanted a son and not a sick and weak wife to drag me down.

This worked very well and Jane agreed to stop seeing her family quite so much. She understood that the contacts was interfering with her duties as a wife and she said that she was going to concentrate very hard on producing a son for our family.

Her friend Joan Stone was soon the only person visiting. Joan and I began a friendship almost as soon as we met. We had much in common including an interest in herbs and their properties. Often we would walk together seeking out special herbs and plants. In the early days of our marriage Jane would accompany us on these jaunts, but as time progressed she insisted that we walk while she rested in her own room. Joan was a very fit girl and so we often ventured further afield to the beach and over to the island to see the remains of the old monastery. I used to scare Joan when I told her about the ghost of smuggler Tom Crocker who haunted the inn and the island. Joan laughed and we fell together on the grass. Joan soon began to tell me of certain incantations which would compel a person to do as they were bid. She was very interesting.

I remember once that I met my father-in-law whilst out walking with Joan and he later told me that this was inappropriate. The upstart of a man telling me, Peter Prideaux, what should be done. I ignored him of course.

By the time Christmas 1688 arrived I was still not a father and most disappointed. Jane cried and apologised as usual and I was not feeling very pleased with her. I had hoped to be holding my son by that Christmas morning.

God obviously had other ideas for us as Jane died of some sort of food poisoning the next day. The doctor was most confused and her family distraught. I found that the event was not quite as upsetting as it might have been.

If I am honest with myself, Jane and I had grown apart in the eighteen months we were together and I had not felt as close to her as I might have done. I was left with the inconvenience of sorting out my affairs once again but found that my lawyer had ensured under my prior instructions that the business was concluded quickly and smoothly.

I married Joan Stone on the 28th May 1689.

This was not as unusual as the local shrews thought as we had so much in common and Joan had been a friend of Jane's and we both felt that it is something that she would have been happy with. We waited until May in order to prevent gossip, although this was not extended to Joan moving away until the wedding. She called at the house as often as she had before and the presence of my loyal staff at the same time gave the local women no cause for concern.

It does amaze me though how a woman becomes so different once she is married. She will literally change as soon as the ring is on her finger. The shy, demure and obedient woman with no view on any subject becomes a harridan who appears to believe that her own opinion matters. Women have so little experience of the world that it is ridiculous for them to imagine that this view could possibly be an informed one.

Joan for example, began to act as though we were in some kind of conspiracy together, asking for extra money for clothes and the like. I no longer felt as though I could go herb hunting with her and took to performing this task alone. I started riding out on my own to the inns of surrounding villages and towns. Modbury was particularly good for meeting fellow gamblers.

My finances were such that it was possible to attend certain clubs in Plymouth where more exciting gambling took place alongside wine and women. I also managed to buy some very fine horses. My life was good except that I was still not a father. Joan seemed less bothered about this than I and told me that a child would arrive soon enough. I however had a position to maintain. Three wives and no children were now beyond a joke and I insisted quite firmly that I should be expecting a child very soon.

I told Joan to take some herbs and she told me in return that her own ministrations to her health were good enough. I could not agree and was sorely disappointed that Joan should speak to me in this way.

I found myself spending more time with my male friends and it has to be said with some female friends while my wife spent a good deal of my money on herself and the house. I agree that the house looked wonderful with its modern furniture and I was never ashamed to bring anyone home and our parties were well attended, very gay and very expensive. I wanted to keep up with my friends and was pleased to be asked to invest in some of the mining ventures proposed.

I was married to Joan for five years until she died of a fall from a horse. She was not a good rider but insisted on riding the feisty mare that day when she accompanied me to visit a mine I had a financial interest in. I did not tell the doctor who attended her, but Joan had been convinced that I was using the rides as an excuse to visit a woman in secret. I challenged her to ride out with me, even choosing her horse and she fell while attempting to jump a hedge after I had already jumped it. She died almost immediately with few words and was buried on the 6th August 1694 in the same Bigbury church where we had been married.

The 20th November 1694 was another happy day, it being the day I married Anne Baron.

Anne was a young woman, sixteen years old, but ready and willing to marry. Her father seemed pleased with my income and property and ignored my age – 43 years old now, I can hardly believe it. Her father was a gentleman with a waning income and I was not adverse to a girl who could produce the son I wanted.

I paid a great deal of attention to Anne and let her have plenty of freedom. This was also to do with the fact I spent a lot of time in town. Three decent marriages had left me well off and I was still able to live the life of a gentleman.

And on the 17th September 1695 Anne produced my son and we named him Peter John.

I was so happy and Anne said that I deserved it after waiting all this time. I was pleased and celebrated so much with my friends that I almost forgot to thank Anne for her part.

Peter was a handsome little chap, but seemed much closer to his mother than to me.

Two years later Ann was born on the 17th May and following two born dead sons, in December 1701 Mary was born. These two daughters did not create the same celebration in the household as Peter had, as I was too busy and had little interest in girls.

Now outnumbered by women, I felt as if I was a stranger in my own house. I had enough of this.

God seemed to hear my complaints because within a month of Mary's birth, all three were dead. Baby Mary first succumbed to a fever, my wife found her dead in the morning. Then two days later four year old Mary was found dead in bed of the same fever. My wife seemed to sicken just after the girls' joint funeral and became depressed and inconsolable. I tried her with all sorts of tempting foods, but soon in mid-January, she too was in the ground on top of our daughters.

My son did not appear to be affected by the traumas and his new young nursemaid took good care of him. It was just after my wife's funeral that I began to notice that I was being treated differently by my friends and neighbours. Conversation stopped as I approached people at parties and some crossed the road and found some important task to take care of if I came anywhere near them.

Then I was summoned for the meeting with Sir William.

He would find no evidence against me as there was none to be found.

It could be asked why I stayed here in this county but the rolling Devon fields, cliffs and waterways are in my blood and I would miss them all if I went anywhere else.

I am startled from my thoughts when Miss Gardener once more enters the room.

"Sir, a note has arrived for you," she says and hands me an envelope. I open it, read it and see that I am summoned yet again to see Sir William. Damned insolence.

I arrive at the hall at twelve the next day. The note said ten, but I am not his servant.

"You are late," says Sir William.

"I am not under arrest. I shall arrive when I please, Sir William."

Sir William stares at me and I am glad that looks cannot kill. Standing next to him is John Potter, his clerk.

"What do you need to see me about today, Sir William? I do have a life apart from visiting you." I smile and this annoys him even more.

"Mr Baron will be here shortly to show me the letter he has which was written to him by your late wife. He has been checking other details which were referred to in the note and will bring all his findings. It seems as though today you shall lose your liberty."

"Is that the reason you have the men sitting in your entrance hall. Are they waiting to arrest me?" He can see I am not taking this seriously.

"Don't try to be so smart Prideaux. I shall have you behind bars by this …"

We are interrupted by one of his men coming into the room carrying a letter.

Sir William opens it and as he reads, I see the colour drain from his face.

"Bad news?" I ask him.

"You are something to do with this aren't you?"

"With what?"

He waves the note in my face and drops it on the floor. Then he storms out of the room.

The clerk reaches it before the note hits the ground and reads it. He looks at me and says, "It appears that Mr Baron died last night."

"Oh that is terrible news," I answer. "How did that happen?"

"It seems that he was perfectly alright after his meal last night and then he went into the study to go through some papers. He was found dead there this morning. As yet they cannot confirm how he died, but initial reports suggest poisoning of some sort."

"Perhaps he has taken his own life. I know he has been very upset by the deaths of my wife and children. He has almost seemed a little unhinged," I say.

I know I must make my point carefully. After all the only reason I am standing here in this room with the clerk of Sir William is because of Baron.

"Yes," says the clerk. He felt quite uncomfortable because he did not know whether this Prideaux man was a mass murderer or a badly maligned person who had suffered dreadful tragedy in his life. The truth could go either way.

"Boo!" I say to the man and he looks startled and runs out of the room.

I look around the room and laugh out loud. Now there would be no further problems for me. A spot of luck my father-in-law dying like that.

When I visited him late last night in his study, my father-in-law had seemed pleased to see me. We talked through the whole situation and after a few drinks of the ale I brought with me; he seemed to come round to my way of thinking. He even started to understand that his daughter, my beloved wife, had been saying many strange things after the death of her daughters. After I tentatively asked to see the letter Anne had written, he was drunk enough to show me. When I read it through twice I realised that in the wrong hands, much could be made of its contents.

I had not known that Anne had spent so much of her time with me recoding all sorts of comments together with lists of herbs and the like.

Clever little Anne.

"I brought you some sweets too John," I said to him. John took and ate them all and soon began to doze peacefully in the armchair. I took my leave and went home.

I did not think that it would be a wise thing to tell anyone else of the visit. No one else had seen me, so I vowed to keep it to myself.

I walk out of the room and find Sir William, his clerk and several men talking in the hallway.

"I shall leave now William," I tell him. "I can't imagine you have any reason to talk to me again." I smile at him and leave by the front door. I can feel his eyes burning into me as I mount my horse.

As I ride home through the woods, I am conscious of a freezing mist which has suddenly dropped. My horse begins to spook and spin and I have to be quite firm with him until he calms down.

"Having trouble with him Sir? He is a fine looking animal."

I look to my left from where the voice comes. I have to say that my heart is racing and my body feels cold and tingly. I am looking at a parson of some sort, although I do not recognise him and I have had quite a bit to do with parsons and the like.

"He is. I think he was surprised to see you walking here. Are you lost?"

"We are all lost," answers the parson.

"Aaaah. You are not trapping me with that kind of talk Parson. I am asking if you are travelling somewhere in particular. I am riding back to my house if you need pointing in the right direction?"

"I know my way, Prideaux. I am wondering if you have any idea where you are going?"

"I just told you, I am going home." Peculiar little man.

"Now you are and yet if I were you, I would worry about where I was going when I die."

"You worry all you like friend. I believe that when you are dead, you are dead. Gone and never to be again."

"Oh no Prideaux. We carry on living and don't ever die and whatever we do causes something to be created in answer to what we have thought or done. Then we must continue another life in the same manner. That is what God does for us and with us."

"Spare me your sermons old man," I am feeling cross about his idiotic speech.

He laughs and throws his head back as he does so.

"Do you miss your mother Peter?"

"That witch left me as soon as she dumped me into this evil life. She left me with an idiot father who did nothing for me. You know Parson, like you I hate women and it started with her." I have no idea why I am telling him this.

"Aaaah, your confession and perhaps the first recognition of your causation."

I stop my horse. I don't need to speak to this man anymore. He is making me feel uncomfortable.

"On your way Parson," I instruct him.

He laughs.

And vanishes into the thick mist.

"Hey!" I shout.

There is no answer and so I assume the old Parson felt that he had warned me of the fate of my eternal soul and has now triumphantly continued his journey into the wood.

The mist is still surrounding us and I feel suddenly aware of mumblings and shadows and extreme ice cold. My horse is standing stock still and almost catatonic – as am I.

I see a group of women ahead of me on the track and shout out to them. The women stop their walk and turn to face me.

"Do you know where the Parson went to?"

They give me no answer and I must assume that they are plain rude. Probably common people.

"You women! Answer me now or I shall ride my horse through you!"

Two children came out from behind the skirts of the women and the dirty little wretches run towards me. The women did nothing to stop them.

"Papa! Papa!" they are saying.

"Where is your Papa?" I ask.

They stop in front of me and stroke my horse. Then in unison they look up to me and say,

"Papa! Why did you kill us all? We didn't harm you and we miss our brother. We miss Peter, we miss Peter!"

They chant and chant and the women join in, "We miss Peter!"

Surely not, surely not! Elizabeth, Jane, Joan, Anne, and little Ann and little Mary? That is not possible. I kick my horse on and ride through the group but they do not scatter as I might expect. They disperse, I mean their bodies disperse into the mist and as I look back from my galloping horse, their bodies reform! They are all holding fingers to their lips. I turn back to the front and do not stop until I reach my village.

When I arrive back home I am met by Miss Gardener.

"Everything alright Sir?" she asks.

"Fine," I answer, smiling at the trusting face.

"I hear Mr Baron was found dead this morning. Did he seem fine when you saw him last night?"

Oh dear. I had thought she was asleep when I left to make the visit. How did she know? I finger the letter and notes I have in my pocket. After considering briefly, I pull them out and give them to Miss Gardener to read.

"I think we should put that rubbish in the fire," she says as she glances over the contents. "Only harm will come from such ridiculous things."

I can see a long future with this girl.

THE RINGMORE WRAITH
featuring Peter Prideaux 1695 – 1749

The first time that Peter saw a ghost was in February 1702, just three weeks after the deaths of his mother and sisters. However, being six, he was not familiar with the concept of a ghost and therefore did not overreact.

He simply liked the young girls who came to his attic room to play with him and the beautiful lady who smelled of flowers and bread. This lady would come to him when he had been locked in his room by either his father or Miss Gardener. When his mother was alive, he had eaten with her and his sister Ann in the nursery until Mary was born. But Mary was so sick and his mother spent all her time with her and so the two elder children had to eat on their own. Then Ann was taken away to the room occupied by mother and baby Mary and Peter did not see any of them alive again.

He saw them once they were dead. His father thought it necessary that Peter should see his dead sisters lying in their shared coffin. He also thought it necessary that he should see his mother on her deathbed and then again in her coffin. When Peter asked his father why they smelled so funny and their faces were all wrinkled and scary, his father told him not to be a fool. They were dead and would soon be buried in the ground and have six feet of soil piled up on top of them and that meant that they could never climb out again because of the weight. He explained that that was why all of those bodies in the churchyard were buried so deep. He also said that if they were not buried with exactly six feet of soil on them, they could climb right out of their graves at night when no one was looking and come round to little boy's bedrooms if they had been naughty and disobeyed their fathers.

Young Peter did not get a proper night's sleep for the rest of his life following this informative lecture.

Miss Gardener was now in charge of his care and she became cruel and neglectful following his mother's death. He was locked in his attic more often than not, this cold, dark space now being used as his bedroom and playroom and dining room.

Miss Gardener and his father spent a great deal of time together during the troubles and for a long while afterwards. Then, gradually things began to change.

Young Peter noticed that as his father spent more time away from the house and away from Miss Gardener, the nastier she became.

Peter was forgotten about on several occasions. He often went without food and water and bathing. One of the maids would sneak up when she could and shout through the locked door,

"Master Peter! Master Peter!"

He would shuffle over to the door sniffling and whispering,

"I am so hungry. Where is Mama?"

The girl quickly unlocked the door and slipped inside.

"Ssssh. You must not say I have been here or I shall lose my place and then there will be no one to help you. Now Master Peter, eat and drink and wash yourself. I will get you some clean clothes from the chest here, but you must not say it is me. She will not notice that that you have been cleaned. I will wash these clothes and bring them back for you to put on again."

Six year old Peter did as he was told and ate and drank quickly. The girl, Matilda Stone, busied herself cleaning the bed and replacing the bedding with fresh from the linen cupboard at the far end of the attic and put all of the soiled garments and linen into a large cotton bag.

"I will wash these at home Master Peter. My mother has heard of the way you are being treated and she is disgusted. She told me to bring you home there, but of course your father will have the law against us."

"I won't say anything," said Peter. "Thank you Matilda."

Matilda smiled a teary smile and rubbed his head.

"I cannot tell you often enough not to tell anyone what I am doing. Just say nothing."

"I won't," he answered and chewed on the toffee she had given him. He felt full and comfortable for the first time in days.

"Cuddle," he said.

Matilda cuddled him and said, "Your mother will be turning in her grave."

Peter looked at with shock upon his face, "Will she climb out and come and save me? I wish she would Matty, I wish she would. I miss her and I want her to come and fetch me from that horrid woman. I want you to look after me."

"I will see what I can do," said Matilda.

It was two nights later when Peter saw his mother for the first time. She said,

"I came before with Ann and Mary, but you only saw us as shadows. We are here properly now."

Peter saw his sisters giggling on the floor as they played with his toy farmyard.

"Did you climb out Mama? Was there not enough soil on you?"

"Plenty of soil Peter my baby boy. Matilda and her mother know some little tricks that have helped me come and help you. But you must not tell anyone."

"No one wants me to tell anyone anything Mama. I don't speak to anyone."

"Does Papa come and see you?" she asked as she stroked his head, already knowing the answer.

"No Mama. I don't think he knows what Miss Gardener does. If he knew how cruel she was, he would save me wouldn't he?"

"Perhaps Peter. But in the meantime say nothing to anyone about anything."

"Never?"

"Never, my darling boy. Mama will always look after you."

His mother cuddled him closer and he slowly drifted off to sleep.

Miss Gardener had her suspicions about Peter Prideaux as soon as they first had sex. It wasn't the first time she had played this game - she had given herself to two previous employers, one in Plymouth and one in Launceston but neither relationship had come to anything. This time she felt that she had a chance of a married existence and a home in which she would be in charge.

In a differing role to the others who had no intention of getting rid of their families on her behalf, Peter appeared to have other ideas. Granted he did not kill his wife for her, but he had killed her nevertheless. Miss Gardener was not bothered over the death of the little girls who had given her several sleepless nights. Miss Gardener believed in the Ten Commandments and as she hadn't actually done the killings, she felt that she was probably safe from eternal damnation.

The little sod Peter, whom his father had told her to look after, was a personified reminder of Mistress Prideaux and the girls and so she did as little as she could for him. Giving instructions to the maids that no one was to attend to him other than herself, she felt as though she would be able to have some control over her destiny. She wasn't really sure how though.

When she did go to see the boy, he would run crying into the corner of the attic and so she slammed food and water on the table and told him to keep his mouth shut. His father never checked on him and rarely asked about him.

Peter Senior just satisfied his primal needs with Miss Gardener without speaking and when she asked about marriage, he answered,

"I am not getting married for the fifth time. They already think I murdered the others and I am not marrying a maid and giving the gossips something else to occupy their boring days."

"I know too much about you Peter. I could tell."

"You tell and you will be in the same place as the others. That is a promise."

So she kept quiet and took out her anger on the boy. Perhaps he too would soon die – perhaps from natural causes.

During the recent few days Miss Gardener had heard noises up in the attic. There was talking and singing and the sound of footsteps running across the floor. Not one set of steps, but several.

At first she had gone upstairs and told the boy off, threatening him with permanent imprisonment. He cried of course and said nothing.

That was another new thing. Peter had stopped speaking to her.

All of this was bad enough, but lately the noises had been continuing through the night. The attic was directly above her bedroom and so although she was not as aware during the day, she could not avoid the noises at night.

Tonight she lay still looking out of her window. It had been a bright night, not a full moon, but bright nonetheless. The clouds were now moving in from the coast and the rumbling in the distance signalled the arrival of a storm. It had been quiet in the attic and Miss Gardener was hoping that Peter would be quieter and quieter until he left the house permanently.

Yes, she could hear it – whispering and laughter. She sat up in bed with her heart beating loudly because she knew that he should be alone. She had checked on him before she retired and found him shivering and sobbing on his bed.

Good - horrible child.

And now there were these noises coming from the attic. She would like to send the maid but having shouted at and hit Matilda, banning her from visiting the child earlier that day - Miss Gardener did not want to back down.

She must go herself.

The night had become much darker and she knew the storm would begin soon. She shivered and drew her wool shawl tight around her shoulders. Her heart still raced with the noises and yet when they stopped she strained her ears to catch them again. It must be the atmosphere of the storm, like when the moon was full and could affect people. She was very jumpy and nervous.

She slapped herself lightly on the face and walked confidently out of the door and up the stairs. She wore slippers and so her traverse was silent. The chattering and squealing from the attic continued and increased and was soon interspersed with running feet and bangs.

As she approached the door, she saw that there were candles lit in the attic and light was dancing across the gap at the bottom. She could see shapes crossing in front of the light and there seemed to be more than one frail child creating them.

She gently opened the door, trying to avoid the creaking sound she knew it made. As she did so, the noises stopped and the lights extinguished. Miss Gardener pushed the door wide and heard whimpering in the room corner as she had when she left earlier.

"What are you doing boy? Waking up the house in the night and where did you get the candles?"

Now she could see that it had all been in her imagination, she stalked over to the bed with her arm raised and prepared to remind the child of who was the boss. The concentration this act required meant that she failed to see what was approaching her from behind.

The blow felled her and it was almost a minute before she felt that she could open her eyes. She was lying on the floor and as the lightning flashed she saw two, perhaps three children playing at the far end, dressed in nightclothes. Standing over her was a woman dressed in a dirty grey and green shroud and who wore long scraggly hair. Her face, reflected in the lightning strike was ghoulish and skeletal.

Miss Gardener whimpered.

"Frightened are you now? You didn't mind my little boy crying out in the dark on his own though, did you?"

"Mrs Prideaux? Is that you? I don't understand what is happening. Am I dead?"

"I am death brought back to life as are my children. Do you want to meet my sister wives? They are here too."

The ghoul seemed pleased with her work and poked Miss Gardener with her bare and dirty foot.

Miss Gardener tried to rise but was unable. The thunder rolled and the lightning struck and if she had had any control over her body at all she would have screamed.

"Come here Peter my boy," instructed Anne Prideaux to her son. This he did and as he crouched down he was joined by his sisters. They all had dark eyes and they moved their heads from side to side as they stared at Miss Gardener.

"What are you going to do to me?" she asked faintly.

"Shall we do what you did to us? Shall we poison you and treat you cruel?"

"I did not poison you, it was Peter. I only knew about it afterwards. And I am sorry about your son, I should have looked after him belter. I am so sorry."

Anne Prideaux answered, "I am not a cruel woman, so I shall not kill you. Instead, I shall ..."

"Mama! I can hear Papa coming! He will beat me again!"

Mama held him closely and Miss Gardener saw her chance.

"He will not beat you ever again. I can see to that. You are dead Mrs Prideaux and unable to protect your son, but I am alive and I can."

This statement appeared to antagonise the phantom and it reared in the air, elongated and open mouthed. Miss Gardener screwed up her eyes and slammed her hands around her ears.

"I want to help, please let me help!" she shrieked. She heard a loud crash and felt suddenly extremely cold.

"What the hell is the matter with you woman?" asked the familiar voice of Peter.

Miss Gardner opened her eyes and answered,

"She was here. Your wife and your daughters. They were here."

She dropped her head on the floorboards sobbing. Peter dragged her upright using her braids.

"They are dead, you ridiculous woman. How can they have been here?" and he slapped her hard, whether from temper or to assist her in her hysterics, it could not be determined.

Miss Gardener rose, if a little unsteadily, to her feet and looked about the room. Young Peter was on the bed, sucking his thumb, but thankfully silent of sobs.

"They were here Peter, they have returned from the grave to protect your son, they said. Mrs Prideaux made me promise to protect him from your beatings or she will make you suffer."

Peter let go of her hair and strode over to his son.

"Is this true?" he asked him.

"Papa, they were here. My Mama and sisters were here with me and they are not buried in the churchyard. I don't think they were buried deep enough and I am so glad."

His father felt rage and fear rise within him, for he realised that if this were so, then there would be too many ghosts. It could not therefore be true.

"Do not speak of this to me or anyone else boy. This is the Devil's work and if you think you see spirits you could be burned as a witch. I would have to tell the parson that you are a witch and they would take you away immediately!"

Young Peter shut his mouth tightly to stop any more words escaping.

"Mr. Prideaux, do not speak to him so! I saw the spirits too and I am no witch!"

Peter ran back to Miss Gardener and kicked her in the stomach and she curled up. The room was silent and freezing and Peter suddenly became uneasy about the moving dark shadows he thought he could see in the attic room corners. His son sat motionless and speechless on the small cot and his housekeeper lay on the floor and was apparently bleeding through her skirt. He thought about dragging her downstairs and finishing her off. If that was a lost child coming from her, then there would be talk and he wanted no more talk.

"Get downstairs you whore and clean yourself up. Once you have done that, I want you to leave this house and never return."

She raised herself up and stared at him,

"But I promised your wife!"

"Promised her what?"

"That I would look after young Peter. If I don't she will attack me again."

"Don't be so ridiculous and get moving."

He ushered her downstairs, disgusted at the blood soaked clothes.

"I have lost the baby I think. It hurts."

He did not answer. He had no intention of producing a base born child in his line. Miss Gardener staggered to her room and shut the door. As she was removing her skirt, she saw the silhouette of Mrs Prideaux backed against the window.

"He is making me leave," Miss Gardener said.

"So I heard, but we are staying here."

"How?"

"You do not need to know how, I know how. The last thing I want you to do is remove the painting from my old room and take it to the attic and hang it over Peter's bed."

"Which painting?"

"I brought it here. It is from my home and is a picture of a stone house and surrounding parkland."

"I know the one, only your husband took it from your room when you died and it is now hidden behind a tapestry in the library."

"All the better, he won't notice it gone. Put it in the attic and tell the boy we are always with him."

The wraith vanished and Miss Gardener busied herself with her dress. Upon hearing a loud bang, she looked out of the window and saw Prideaux galloping away. She ran out of the room and downstairs to the back kitchen and quickly recovered the painting. She dragged it with difficulty until she met Matilda in the passage.

"We need to take this to Master Peter to keep him safe."

"You saw his mother? Did she punish you?"

Miss Gardener stopped her efforts and looked at the girl,

"Matty, I have just this last half hour miscarried my baby. I have been punished."

Matilda nodded and helped her former enemy with the painting and they soon had it installed on the attic wall. The still silent boy looked at it and cuddled his pillow.

"We should get him a dolly or a toy bear or something," said Matilda.

"You can, I have been told to leave today and never return."

"Why?"

"Because he is a coward and he doesn't want me here because I know…"

"You know what Miss?"

"I know what sort of a man he is and if I tell anyone, he will kill me."

Miss Gardener patted the boy on his head and said to Matilda,

"Look after him and keep the picture there and don't move it until Peter or his mother tells you to."

She swished out of the room and Matilda almost felt sorry for her. She examined the picture carefully as she dusted it. It was a very large oil painting of a stone mansion with lawns to the front and side and trees and shrubs circling it. It was a night scene and the full creamy moon had the edges of clouds surrounding it. The house windows were in darkness and the impression was one of sleep and comfort.

Matilda stroked Peter and said,

"I will look after you young man and I will fetch you food and clean clothes, now don't you worry."

Peter looked at the painting after Matilda left and surveyed the scene. He saw the house and the moon and the trees and the people standing in front of the house waving at him. There were lights at all the windows and the open front door revealed a warm and cosy hallway. A lady and two girls stood and waved and blew kisses and there, walking across the lawn were three more ladies who turned and waved too.

"You are safe Peter. We shall always watch over you!" they shouted.

He snuggled back under his blankets as Matilda returned with food.

"Eat this Peter and then go to sleep. You can have a bath and change your clothes in the morning."

Matilda glanced at the painting and muttered,

"Oh! I didn't see the people before. That's funny; they look like your mother and sisters."

The figures waved to Matilda and she stepped back at first shocked and then pleased.

"They are looking after you Peter," she said.

*

Peter never spoke a word again to a living soul. He relied on the picture to keep him sane and happy throughout his childhood and when he was finally allowed into a room of his own and had a tutor, he took the painting with him. His father did not notice as Matilda made the arrangements, ensuring that it was hung directly over his bed.

The tutor was brought in to help the boy learn as much as a mute could. Peter read most of the books in the library without commuting this fact to anyone other than Matilda and of course, the picture wraiths.

Initially Mama would climb out in order to rock him to sleep and his sisters would come and play with him and Matilda brought him his food and clean clothes. Later Mama helped him to read and study and learn how to behave like a gentleman. His sisters, who had remained a steady 10 years of age in direct conflict to the age they were when they died, taught him to dance and held competitions in many subjects. The previous wives, who visited the painting and therefore him, were a jolly trio who showered him with love and often gave aunt like assistance.

These women he did not need to speak to. They all understood through thought and Peter remained self-involved and ventured outside rarely.

His father rarely visited him, instead choosing to spend his time in ale houses and gambling. His fortune was diminishing and his investments bringing in little. He must bring in more income if he did not want to downsize his living standards in any way.

He decided that smuggling was to be his answer and agreed to allow hidden storage at their Ringmore home.

"I shall invest in the business if I make money from this involvement," he told a fellow gambling companion.

"You are doing this to pay off your debts and if I decide, you will be involved more. As soon as you have paid me off then we shall see about investment."

Peter Senior was finding it difficult to acknowledge the problems he was facing.

As the strange men arrived at their house during the night, bringing contraband which was to be stored in hidden cupboards and rooms latterly used during the

Civil War, Peter and Matilda would leave the house and go down to the beach.

They would watch the men arrive in their boats and see the clippers far out to sea. They liked listening to the men panic or boast about their exploits. The beach was only minutes away from the house and no one noticed a mute boy and a tiny maid only five years older than he.

Mama had visited with them on a few occasions and the girls and his adopted aunts would come when they were sure the beach was empty. But it was too much of a picnic when they all attended and ran about.

And there was no swimming. The women would not enter the water.

"We can travel on the water in a boat," Mama informed her son.

"We would need a big boat," answered Peter.

"Not if you brought the picture," said Mama. "Then we could all row along the coast and see the sights."

So they chose a night when they could row between tides and stay in the shadows of a moonless night. Matilda put the painting in an old hand cart after wrapping it in a sack. She had added the usual food they liked to take, only for Peter and her, naturally. The run to the beach was all downhill and so the load easy. They were not thinking about the return journey.

Matty had chosen which boat they would take and they climbed into it, heaved the painting behind a seat and pushed the boat out of the shallows. The sound of the smooth calm incoming tide was relaxing. As Peter moved the oars in the dark water, he noticed how the sea seemed much thicker than stream water. He pondered the idea as they rowed further out to sea before heading west towards the mouth of the Erme.

"Let's go to Mothecombe and nose around there," said Mama from the lawn bench on which she sat in the front of the picture. The painting was propped up against a seat and secured by thin rope, to enable the women to view their night-time trip.

The water was so calm that they were able to see the lamps in cottage windows on the shore and the only sound from the sea was the waves slapping against the boat side. As they rowed around the headland, Peter noticed that the sea was becoming a little choppy but put it down to the changing tide.

They rowed across the estuary in order to reach the Mothecombe side and soon learned that this was a serious error when the rowing boat began rocking from side to side in a violent manner.

Matty said, "Peter, I think that this is getting a bit dangerous."

"Peter, you must not be alarmed but you must get us all to the shoreline. If you lose this painting, then we must stay here forever." His mother clearly trying to keep her family calm was failing miserably.

Peter was more than aware of the danger they were in. The idea of a row to Mothecombe, where he had visited with his aunt when he was younger had sounded so exciting. The thought that he could visit with his mother and sisters made it even better. Now the sea was frightening and the boat rocking and he really did not know what to do next.

White tops appeared on previously invisible waves and Matty and Peter had to hold tight onto both sides of the boat to save themselves from falling in. The oars had already dropped into the sea and the painting was wobbling dangerously from side to side. With the exception of his mother, the women were screaming in loud pitched voices.

Matty grabbed Peter's arm and pointed to the bobbing heads of seals surrounding the boat. He stared, unable to appreciate their beauty.

"Hello!" said a seal.

Peter stopped his panicking for a moment and watched the seal as she raised herself over the side of the boat. It was obvious she was a woman as her bare breasts were raised over the boat side as she held on, using her bent arms.

Matty squealed and said,

"You are a mermaid, aren't you? You are so pretty. I love mermaids!"

"Do you know many mermaids?"

"Well no! I have just heard the stories about you. I would love to be your friend."

"Funny little girl. I see that you have some spirit women who are in distress."

Peter put a protective arm over the painting as he saw his mother and sisters holding each other as they rocked and fell from the bench upon which they had been sat. His aunts were lying next to a large oak tree to which they held on for apparent dear life.

"You are a mute boy, aren't you? Many of us cannot speak where I live either, we don't need to."

The maid dragged herself higher onto the boat and Peter could see that she was naked from the waist up and was wearing some kind of pale green and blue shimmering garment below. Although still dark, he was surprised to note that he could still see the colours.

"Don't worry about the sea and the waves. We will look after you and your spirit family. It is they who drew us to you."

A giggling and splashing made them look behind the maid. There were several others, similar to their boat visitor and they were carrying seaweed which they began wrapping around the rowlocks.

Soon, the maids were pulling them towards the beach.

"Mothecombe Beach is very quiet. You can stay here until the tide turns and then paddle back to your own beach."

"I am Matilda and this is Peter Prideaux," said Matty, once they were safely ensconced with their boat on the dry sand. The mermaids had arranged themselves on the rocky outcrop at the beach edge and their tails splashed and kept contact with the water. They were beautiful creatures and their tails, much bigger than one might imagine, were covered in large rainbow coloured scales. They had tail fins, but these seemed to be intertwined with a floating rainbow like dress material.

They were naked, but their bodies were covered in long wavy hair and their laughter and graceful movements proved they were anything but ashamed or embarrassed of their undressed state.

Peter's mother, sisters and aunts were having the time of their lives running along the beach and squealing and shrieking.

"I wish we could stay here forever," said little Mary.

"You can if you wish," answered the mermaid.

"How?" asked Anne Prideaux.

"If you follow us into the sea, all you spirit people, down to where we live, you will be able to live in and by the sea forever."

"Will we not drown mother?" asked little Ann.

"No daughter, that is not possible. If we live by the sea and swim under the sea, we shall never be able to return to the picture. That is what it means Mistress Mermaid?"

"It is. We are all restless spirits under water, we cannot return to the land and spirits on land cannot go into the sea. It is your choice, but there will be no more living in a painting at the beck and call of only one person."

Peter looked up. The mermaid meant him.

"I wish to be near to my son and protect him from his murderous father."

"He is old enough to fend for himself now Anne. He will be forced to leave the family home soon when his father loses it."

Peter stood up and walked over to his mother. He was not able to hold back his tears, but he knew that he must release her from her prison and by letting her go, he would be able to leave too.

"We can all visit with each other anytime we want," said his mother. "The girls need to be able to get out and about now."

Peter nodded and after a few farewells, watched his erstwhile family walk happily into the sea. His mother turned and waved and blew him a kiss as she waded into the dark water. Matty reached for his hand and held it tightly as the spirits vanished into the water.

"Come on Peter. We have got to get back before it gets light again."

Peter helped push the boat back out to sea and jumped in after Matty. They began to row back across the river mouth towards the Red Cove side and encountered such rough water that they nearly lost the mermaid returned oars again. Before they were halfway across the estuary a head bobbed up and then another and then another.

"Peter! Look" We have tails! We can swim!"

And there they all were, swimming and splashing and happy.

"No one ever dies Peter. It is not possible!" And the laughing group pulled the rocking boat back to their launch site below Ringmore. There were two early fishermen busy at the water's edge.

"You youngsters better get back quick as you can. If Alf Pike finds you've had his boat out, he will clip your ears, Prideaux or no Prideaux," said one.

"Who is that in the water? One of your friends?" said his companion.

"Mermaids," answered Matty.

"Clear off or I will clip your ears," said the fisherman.

Peter and Matty ran up the hill away from the beach and when they looked back they could see the surface of the sea greatly disturbed with a patch moving south. Matty dragged Peter's arm and they began their homeward journey with hand trolley and half empty painting.

One of the fishermen said, "Pointless going out this morning now. Those damn mermaids will have taken the fish with them." And he bad temperedly threw his pots out of the boat.

*

In 1749 on a warm night in April, Peter took an early walk down to Aymer Cove using the track from his house. He enjoyed sitting on the pebbles and watching the sea.

He did this on as many mornings as he could and often in the early hours, as he had great difficulty sleeping.

He had five children, the eldest 20 and the youngest only 10. There had also been three dead babies and those losses had affected his wife very much. She was a difficult woman to live with and the fact that Peter never spoke and could only nod his head and offer mild pats in comfort, probably did not assist her recovery.

Peter hadn't married until his early thirties because he had needed to build a career as a carpenter when his father died shortly after losing their family home to his bankers. The only property they had left was a large house near Noddon Mill complete with land and orchards, for which his father had been given the 99 year lease on the 19th December 1698. Francis Kirkham the previous tenant, had died after falling into the mill pool late one night, apparently drunk and was found early the following morning. There had been rumours that Francis was owed a good deal of money by Peter Prideaux, but it could not be proven. Funnily enough it was this same pool where Miss Gardener was found dead, shortly after leaving her employ with the Prideauxs. It was said that she killed herself as there was evidence that she had recently lost a child and she knew that she would have been scorned.

Young Peter was 24 years old when his father finally died. He awoke after hearing screaming in the middle of the night and upon looking out of his bedroom window to the orchard, for this was from where the screaming came, saw his father in a nightshirt running towards the mill. Peter was sure that he could see a mist in pursuance of him. By the time Peter had run downstairs and found his father, he was face down in the stream, his legs in a fearsome animal trap.

He had such a look on his face that the women who laid him out and washed him said he must have died in dreadful fear.

Matty, her brother and his wife all worked for them and between them took care of the house, the animals and the land. The only money earned was that which was earned at market. John was also a carpenter and it was he who taught Peter his early carpentry skills, which Peter then elaborated upon throughout his life to eventually become a most sort after craftsman.

Peter had managed to stay in the house and smallholding and lived in comfort with his dogs and a few animals. There were plenty of young girls calling on him with pies and offers of help for a man could not manage alone, but these were all rejected. Peter had had enough of women.

It hadn't taken him long to put out of his mind the events of his childhood. The memories were terrible enough but the actions of his unhinged father gave Peter plenty to focus on. After his death, Peter had insisted that his father be buried one foot lower than usual so that he would never climb out. Rector Thomas Heskett had wanted to have Peter Senior buried with his wife in order to save valuable space in the churchyard, but Peter paid extra to have him buried at the far end of the grounds.

He didn't climb back out and Peter had not been seen since. He had however seen many others walking around Ringmore and its narrow roads waving to him as they visited their old families and watched from the fence lines. Sometimes he would see them walk down to the beach on which he now sat. It was so much easier to see spirits when their glowing mist form was viewed against the dim and dark light of the night. Sunshine often cancels out the phantoms to the uninitiated.

The familiar splashing and high pitched squealing sounds carried across the water and Peter jumped up. He waved and his mother and sisters waved back.

"Come, come Peter! The night is wonderful!"

So he pushed a boat onto the water, now his own boat, and rowed over to his family.

This made him happy – being with them. Much more so than his own family which was an odd concept. He put it down to his unusual upbringing and his inability to feel love and affection for anything other than his dogs. He had been shown so little affection during his life that to give love to a person seemed strange. He was kind and helpful and aware of his responsibilities. His family had never gone without food and they enjoyed living in a decent house with an excellent reputation.

He wasn't enjoying his life lately though. He often felt as though a heavy black ceiling was above him and he couldn't raise his energies or enthusiasm high enough to move it. Over the years he had discovered that he used the least energy if he left the ceiling above his head until it moved of its own accord. Life was just too long and difficult and now his dog had died.

George had sickened suddenly over the past couple of weeks and he had done everything he could for him. He had stopped his work in order to care for him and sent his son instead. It seemed that his contractors were happy with the temporary replacement and so Peter was able to spend every waking minute with George - the most faithful dog a man could have.

Peter had initially been suspicious of his wife as she had no love of dogs and resented one in her home. Peter believed that she may have been poisoning him and it brought back too many memories. But Joan was genuinely upset about George's illness and looked after the dog while Peter slept.

Then last night George died. He licked his master's hand and howled as he fell back into his basket.

Peter didn't cry, because he never cried. And now his life was over.   He was 54 and didn't want to start again with another George.

He pushed the boat further out until he was waist deep in the water and then pulled himself into it. He had a surge of sadness as he thought of all the times George would have been waiting for him in the boat, wagging his tail and barking at his silly master.

Peter rowed towards the splashing and saw his mother and sisters swimming in the warm moonlight.

They looked as young as ever and welcomed him as they always had when he visited. He never brought his wife or his children to the beach and they left him to his night-time ramblings.

As he rowed nearer, he heard an almighty thunder crack which had been preceded by a lightning flash Then nothing.

Peter looked back to shore and noticed that a thick green mist obscured his view of the land. It would no doubt clear before long.

He reached for his oar and heard a bark.

It was George.

Peter reached out for his friend and George licked his hand and wagged his tail. His mother leaned over the side of the boat and stroked George as she always did. George jumped off the boat and swam along with the mermaids. Peter went to grab him, fearful of him drowning and then remembered that he had buried George only a few hours earlier.

Perhaps he hadn't buried him deep enough.

George swam away and then turned and barked at Peter and under the applause of his family, Peter jumped in too.

He now saw that the mist had moved seaward and covered his boat, but it didn't matter.

As Peter swam strongly towards Mothecombe with his family and his dog, he thought that his wife would not have to worry about how deep he was buried.

.

THE LANLIVERY LIGHTS
featuring Peter Prideaux 1733 – 1810

The document detailed below was written by Mary Prideaux, wife of Peter Prideaux following his death in 1810. It was discovered in her desk drawer by her son Thomas Peter Prideaux who became known as Teepee, for ease of address.

I have reproduced it word for word as I am able to read it – some of the pages have been spoiled over the years.

This is the life story of my husband Peter Prideaux and because of the years we have spent together is also my life story. Some of the facts I have taken from the questions I asked his and my family but most Peter told me or I already knew. Some of the story may appear to be in the form of a confession, but I want only to put my side of the story. I told him many times that he should record such an interesting life and he said he would do so when he had nothing better to do. He is now in the ground at Modbury church and so I have decided that before I join him, I shall write these stories down in case one of our ancestors may be interested.

Being fifteen when your father dies is very difficult for anyone and young Peter was no exception. He and his father had never been close but Peter thought of his childhood as happy and carefree.

His mother and father got on well together, although his father was a mute and only communicated by signal and written notes. The family only realised after his death that they knew little about his younger life apart from the gossip which persisted about his grandfather. I think that is also why I wanted to make sure that my Peter's personal history is known.

On the night his father died, he was noticed by an early fisherman climbing into his boat and rowing out to sea. Then he was seen jumping out of the boat and swimming away. The fisherman thought he saw dolphins or sharks splashing around him and it was assumed that he drowned while trying to escape from them. His body was never found, but that wasn't an uncommon occurrence on that coastline.

It had meant a deal of trouble for the young Prideaux family when it was certain that the breadwinner would not be returning home. There was very little money left and so my Peter had to actively pursue unpaid accounts. Most were paid immediately and more work given to him. The community did not want the family to starve and helped where they could.

"I promise I will complete the work that my father promised to do. I have finished my apprenticeship and will get in help if I need to," he pleaded with them.

A few refused outright, not wishing to trust their jobs to such a young man, but some agreed to let him continue the jobs - at a reduced rate of course.

But he earned enough to keep the family fed and the youngest boy helped with the lighter and less complicated jobs. The eldest Joan went to work for a local farmer and his mother but was sent home when she became pregnant by him, although he denied touching her. The family suffered the shame of the arrival a base born son but the kind Rector Thomas Heskett, one of the longest serving holy men ever at All Hallows, did agree to baptise little John in order to insure him against a fiery eternity.

Peter made the errant seducer pay a few months later when he met him walking alone along the coast path by the cove one night and ensured he would not father another child.

After building up his new business for a couple of years, Peter was engaged to work on the house in which his father was born. This was the house which had been repossessed by his creditors.

"We should do well with this job mother," he said as he set off. "The house is very well built and the timber I have been given to work with is good oak. There is a porch to be built and carving to be done."

"Will you tell them who you are?" she asked.

"They already know mother. How could they not?"

"I gather that they are strangers from the north and may not yet have been told the history of the house."

"Somerset is hardly the north mother, but I take your point."

Peter had been practising on pieces of wood in his father's workshop. The feel of the wood and the tools with which he would make pictures on it, drew praise from anyone who saw it. He hoped he would make a great impression when he did the work.

He arrived at the house and walked directly to the front door. Young Peter had always loved the confident ability of his father to do this and be made welcome. It was not easy to get a master craftsman such as Peter Prideaux and so he was always looked after. My Peter hoped that he would have the same success as his father in this regard.

The current owner, Mr Fox, was aware that Peter's father and grandfather had once lived here. He was far too much of a gentleman to make comment however.

"Do you think you could have a look up there for me Peter? I have been thinking of getting carving along the timbers. What do you think? Go and have a look." said Mr Fox.

"I will sir. Though I am not sure how obvious any sort of carving would be. No one will see it."

"It would be visible from the balcony and I want this to be the most beautiful house in the neighbourhood!"

Peter moved the ladder over to the side of the house and made sure that it was safely in position.

"Shall I hold it for you Peter?" asked Mr Fox.

"No, I will be alright. You can go about your own work sir."

Mr Fox watched his young man move quickly up the ladder and begin to examine the timber above the attic floor windows. He moved away and walked towards the load of oak which was being delivered and addressed William Freeman.

"Hello William. I did not know that you were coming here today."

"I am just delivering some wood and stuff for all this building that is going on. I have to get back to town quickly though and bring back more. This job must be costing you a fortune!"

"Well don't complain. It is keeping you lot in work!"

"I won't. See you later Mr Fox."

William clicked to his pony and it trotted off, pulling the now empty cart around the corner of the house.

Edward Fox watched them trot off and he turned away. Suddenly he heard a tremendous crash followed by the sound of shouting and he saw men run towards the noise. He ran too, already dreading what may have happened. He came around the corner and saw a tangle of pony, cart and ladder.

The pony got up and stood still, apparently safe. Two men lay on the ground, neither moving. Mr Fox ran to the men and looked at the still body and staring eyes of William Freeman. Peter Prideaux was face down and unmoving.

"Come on sir. There is nothing you can do here," said one of the other men.

Fox pulled back and turned Peter over. Instinctively he thumped him in the chest and shouted, "Breathe!"

Two days later he attended the funeral of William Freeman and the sickbed of Peter Prideaux.

Edward Fox said that he was very sorry but he would have to get in another carpenter, now that my Peter was suffering from a broken leg and ribs. Peter could not be expected to take on the responsibility of such a big job on his own but he promised that he would recommend Peter for smaller jobs. He would also look out for some on his own estate.

This downturn in income affected the standing of the family greatly, especially when his mother and sister were forced to take in washing in order to meet the household bills while Peter recovered.

Peter wondered whether to mention to his mother about the sight which had met his eyes when he first climbed the ladder to reach the attic window. He never told her but did tell me one night when he was feeling a bit down.

He said he saw a little boy sobbing on a small cot in the corner of the attic. That did not seem right or appropriate and he determined to ask Mr Fox about him as soon as he was back on the ground.

He tapped on the window in order to get the boy's attention and give him comfort in some way. The boy looked at him and stopped sobbing for a while. Then he saw a woman dressed in grey seemingly jump from a painting on the wall and scoop the boy into her arms. Just as Peter was going to knock again, he noticed children jumping from the painting and land softly on the attic floor. Surely it must be a window – or a hatch?

As he pondered this conundrum he was utterly shocked when a woman's face appeared on the other side of his window. The face was ghoul like and green and the black eyes peering through the straggly hair burned into Peter's mind. He felt his senses smoke and his head spin. At the same moment he heard a crash and saw the ladder wobble and sway.

Before he fell, he saw more phantoms at the window laughing and pointing at him. Peter remembered nothing else until he looked into the eyes of Edward Fox as he came back from the dead.

His mother never recovered from the shock of his accident and the shame of their position and her health rapidly deteriorated until she could only sit in front of the fire and stare. Peter managed to get on his feet quite quickly and with the aid of a pair of crutches and strong will he disguised his serious pain and made chairs and tables in his workshop. These sold well and kept the bills paid until he was able to take on more serious jobs.

Joan finally died following years of poor health, on Peter's 23rd birthday and he arranged her burial within two days. He knew that she had died of a broken heart. I remember how sad the family was, but I was only five years old at the time. That seems odd when I think back although it has never mattered really.

Thomas, Peter's younger brother worked alongside Peter. Thomas was married but Peter did not bother with women. Responsibility was weighing heavy on him and he didn't want a wife and children for a while yet. That is what he told me years later, but I know for a fact that he had lots of girls.

Other local girls made plays for him and some he took up on their offers, but none were able to lead him to the altar. He saw Joan, Elizabeth, Ann and Thomas marry and begin families, but Peter was not tempted. He took girls to the nearby beach and into the woods, but never lost his heart.

He was plagued with dreams and fancies about the past. Work came in regularly and he could easily provide for a family now, but all he wanted to do was travel, not into unknown lands, but back to Cornwall where he felt very strongly that his roots lay.

Peter was well read and spent much of his time learning as much as possible. He asked questions of anyone whom he thought he might know and became quite an expert on the history of Devon and Cornish families.

He was quite sure that the Prideauxs could be traced prior to the Norman invasion, but had so far found it impossible to make the links. Some of his information had come from father to son and he felt that often this information was more reliable than that which was written by those who had no knowledge of the people about whom they were writing. Peter had been feeling this way since he had seen the phantoms in the attic.

Knowing a little of his recent ancestors, he was sure they were connected to him.

Sometimes he imagined that he had become more knowing since that day, when he nearly died. Or had died, if he paid any attention to what the other workmen were inclined to say.

His mother certainly thought that he was different after the accident, but would have been surprised to learn that since that day he often saw his dead family in addition to other friends and neighbours who had passed.

Peter would choose to visit Aymer Cove as he saw fewer people there than at Challaborough. He would often see large fish out at sea. If pressed he would have said mermaids, but felt more comfortable mentioning ghosts than mermaids. So he told no one.

My family - the Wills family were particular friends of the Prideauxs. We lived in one of the cottages between the Prideaux property by the mill and Ringmore village. They often talked to each other over a drink in the evening at the Inn.

My father Thomas, found Peter to be a very clever man and enjoyed spending time with him. My mother Annie had a serious crush on Peter before I was born and would try and seduce him whenever she could engineer that they were alone together. All that had come of it was a kiss and that he regretted especially as Annie reminded him of it whenever she saw him. He told me this story years later when he was a little drink sodden. I didn't mind but I had a horror that he was about to tell me that he had discovered that I was his daughter as well as his wife. Thankfully this was not so. It might seem a strange thing to say but I know of two – no three people who have the same father and grandfather and also marriages which have taken place between brother and sister when parental origins had not been completely brought into the open. I have been told that baptism wipes away all problems in this regard but I don't understand how that can be so.

When I was fifteen years old I began to take a shine to the dark haired, dashing Peter Prideaux. I was at the silly age that I have recognised in our own daughter. Because of the way I behaved, I looked after our girl too much and she resented me for it.

I went round one evening to see Peter and bring him a birthday present. An excuse of course, I had ensured that he would be on his own and that we were unlikely to be disturbed. His housekeeper was at her sister's and the other servants had finished work or gone to the inn.

The night was dark and ideal for paying a visit to a friend which I did not want recorded. I clutched the embroidered waistcoat which I had been working on for months and was now wrapped in cream linen.

"Mary this must have cost you a fortune. I can't accept this."

"I was given the material by Mistress Stone; I just did the needlework myself. Do you like it?"

He told me later that my eyes had bewitched him and that night he could not see beyond those and forgot my age and innocence. I have come to see later that was his excuse to take advantage of me. But I was too young back then.

"Come on in the cottage silly and have a drink and a piece of cake. My sister brought me some food today."

"That is because you never bother for yourself. I would bother for you," I said in my practised shy voice. I followed him into the house and busied myself cutting cake and pouring ale, a task I had seen my mother perform for my father.

After performing a few more personal tasks for him, he said,

"Come on Mary. You had better get yourself home now."

I felt grown up, ashamed and conscious that I could never go back on what had just happened. It hadn't felt special or lovely or anything like that. I didn't even feel as close to him as I had when I first arrived at his door.

"Don't tell anyone about what we have just done," was all Peter said to me.

So I smiled, left his house and went home. In the weeks that followed, I hardly saw him, let alone spoke to him.

As I got fatter from what I thought was depression and overeating, Peter took himself off to Cornwall to take on a big job a friend had set up for him.

He told me all about a few years after we were married.

At The Crown Inn in Lanlivery, Peter stopped for sustenance and a bed.

"What is your business 'ere my lovely?" asked the bonny girl who served him.

"I am working locally for as few months and need board and lodging until I can find a cottage with a workshop."

"I can find you a bed 'ere. What is your name?"

"I am Peter Prideaux of South Devon."

"Well now!" she stopped pouring the cider and stood with her hand on her hip, as might be expected of a woman such as she.

"John, John come over here! We have one of your Devon relatives in tonight!"

This John Prideaux turned out to be a very friendly and influential man in Bodmin. Peter was made so welcome that he would normally have felt quite embarrassed about the attention.

"Now why have you come to visit us?" John asked.

Peter told him about the house on which he had been contracted to work and that he would be in the area until at least Christmas and needed a cottage to rent.

"You must meet my grandfather," he said and called over a very old man who had just entered the inn.

"Grandad, meet Peter Prideaux from Devon. He is working on the Old Manor and needs a place to stay for a few months."

William, the grandfather took Peter's hand and stared into his eyes.

"We have met before Peter," he said.

Peter suddenly felt very strange and wondered if it was the ale he had been drinking. He felt as though his head was swimming as he realised that the two of them were standing in a forest surrounded by men he did not recognise.

"Oh, have we?" he answered.

"I'll come with 'ee on the next part of your trip Peter. Come to my house tonight and we shall talk."

So Peter did as he was bid and was glad of it.

William showed Peter into the pretty cottage at Lanlivery after they had put the pony into a stable. It was warm inside but quite dark. William went over to the hearth and rattled the fire with a poker until he brought it back into life. He took the lamp, lit the wick and put it into the centre of the table.

"Sit down 'ere Peter and make yourself at home."

Peter sat on a wooden settle which was placed at right angles to the fire and leant forward towards the flames. He took the bowl which had been handed to him and sipped it. Hot soup was not quite what he expected, but he enjoyed it nonetheless.

"I will show you where you are sleeping in a minute Peter. Then tomorrow we shall talk about things."

William took Peter up the rickety steps and into a tiny room at the top of the stairs.

"I sleep here in the room on the right and you on the left," he said.

Peter lay on the small bed and wondered what age of small child it had been made for. He curled up his legs, covered himself with the patchwork covers and fell into a deep sleep. He was awakened by a noise which he initially assumed was his host calling him down for breakfast. It was still dark but Peter got up quickly not wishing to cause offence. He was downstairs before he realised that William was still in bed and it was only 2, according to the ticking clock.

Peter decided he would fetch some milk from the pitcher he had seen in the back kitchen and check on his pony. As he walked outside, the time was confirmed as he heard the hall clock chime twice. His pony was asleep, flat out on straw and perfectly content. Peter took a walk to the front of the cottage and stood in the lane watching contentedly the sleeping cottages.

He leant against the cottage and lit his pipe. He noticed flickering lamp lights over in the church yard initially and assumed that they belonged to early workers, possibly mine workers. The lights came across the cemetery and stopped at the wall which divided it from the lane. Peter looked forward to meeting the men as they passed through the lych-gate. But they never arrived. Peter saw the lamps reach the gate, the light hiding full detail of the shadows and then the lights extinguished.

Peter waited a moment and then his curiosity got the better of him. He went over to the gate and walked through it. He noticed an icy rain feeling which engulfed him as he did so but noticed nothing else. There was no one there.

Peter walked back to the cottage, nervously checking behind him every few steps.

The next morning dawned bright and clear and Peter came downstairs to find his host already making breakfast. Breakfast consisted of meat and egg and bread. Peter had not realised how hungry he was and ate quickly.

William ate also, but more slowly. He looked at Peter closely and said,

"You look just like the rest – handsome, strong and with those dark eyes. You are a seeker and look for information everywhere. You want to know it all in an instant. And you can see spirits."

Peter mentioned what he had seen in the night.

"Seen them already have you?" and he laughed.

"Seen who? Are you saying they were ghosts? And what do you mean by all the rest? Like whom?" asked Peter bewildered.

"We descend from a special people Peter and are always interacting with ghosts and phantoms and all sorts of strange things."

Peter said nothing. He felt uncomfortable about the content of William's speech.

"I will go with you to the Old Manor if you like. I could do with a trip out."

Peter agreed. He guessed that it might be useful to have a local man accompany him when he turned up for the job. This work had come from a recommendation from Mr Fox who still felt guilty about Peter's fall and sent work his way whenever he was able. The owner of the Old Manor, Mr Hele wanted panelling and carving in several rooms in the house including the grand staircase. Peter was nervous and he didn't mind saying so.

They tacked up William's pony and attached the cart, complete with his tools. They first pulled into the Crown Inn and spoke to the smith at the forge next to it.

William shouted over to him,

"Hello Tom, how are you? "

"Hello William. Who is the stranger with you?"

William brought Peter over to meet Tom who looked at him closely and said, "Oh I see, another one." And he went back to his work.

William went into the Crown to do whatever business he needed to do and Peter looked at the men and horses that were waiting for Tom the smith. One came over to talk to him.

"I used to work in the mine over at St Blazey but I lost my job there," he said after discovering that Peter was working locally.

"Oh dear why?"

"I complained about working conditions. No one does that. You don't need an assistant do you? I could do with some money."

"Are you a carpenter?"

"Twenty years man and boy down that pit sir. I am a very good and skilled carpenter if you need one."

"I will know better once I have seen the job. What is your name sir?"

"My name is Zeb Prowse. I live in the village and can be found quite easily."

"I will certainly keep you in mind. Are the conditions at the mine so bad?"

"There was a terrible accident there about twenty years ago. Six men from this village and surrounding area were killed including my father and two uncles."
"I am very sorry to hear about that Zeb."

Zeb touched his hat and walked away as William hobbled towards the cart.

"We need to get on our way William."

"Yes we do," he said and clambered aboard.

They travelled along the shaded byways. Peter guessed that these lanes were narrower than the lanes in Devon; they went past a small river running alongside the road.

"When the rain is falling during the winter, that stream is a torrent. The tinners used it to wash the ore and get the tin out, back in the day. Because of that practice, eventually the estuary silted up and now the sea does not come up so far. Not so very long ago, the water was right up to Pontsmill and different valleys around here had ships coming right up. Now it is only land and the ships can no longer get here," said William.

"Do you know, I was thinking that this place would have had more connection with the sea. I keep imagining that I will see someone I know, but I don't know how that is possible."

Warming to the theme, he added, "I really feel as though I have been here before."

"You have, in a manner of speaking. Wait until I show you the castle."

"Castle?"

William stopped talking now that he had Peter's full attention and stared straight ahead smiling. Every so often he gave instructions about which way to turn, up a lane, down a lane, all the time surrounded by woods and ferns, moss and bracken. They travelled through Luxulyan, a village which Peter promised himself that he would have a proper look at on the return journey. The valley out of Luxulyan was other worldly and Peter imagined he saw faces peering at him from behind trees and boulders.

"This is a beautiful place," remarked Peter.

"Aye it is. When I die, I shall come here and stay."

Peter thought that this was a peculiar remark to make, but on reflection he agreed. If there is a choice after death, then this would be a good place to spend eternity.

They continued up the steep, rock strewn path in silence and straight along when the road levelled until it began to drop down when suddenly, William told him to stop and down he jumped.

"Tie the pony up, we shall walk the rest of the way."

They had arrived by a track in the wood which led steeply uphill. First they crossed a stream by way of a log which had fallen conveniently over it. Peter thought he heard chanting or singing.

"Is there a monastery hereabouts?" he asked.

"Oh, hearing it already are you? No, there is no monastery here," laughed William and Peter asked nothing more. William was going to play with him today and Peter did not fancy being played with.

They climbed up the steep track further into the wood where the sky was only visible through the roof of the tree canopy and elsewhere the sun streamed through the trees intermittently. The track turned one way and then the other, all the time taking them skyward. There were small stone walls alongside the track which were covered in lichen and moss.

They scrambled over a wall and followed the track to where there were fewer trees and the land rose steeply. While Peter felt a little out of breath, William was not affected.

"See here and here. This is where the entrance would have been - well one of the entrances. Follow me and keep up!"

William seemed to climb faster and Peter caught up as William stood on yet another stone wall. Part of this wall was covered with grass and soil and was more than a little ramshackle.

"Up you get slowcoach. You a young man too!" William said laughingly.

Peter was not prepared for what he saw when he stood on the top of this wall. The wall was a large circle, no not a circle - an oval. It circumnavigated the summit save for two breaks where it was possible to enter and leave without climbing. Many of the stones were missing, removed no doubt by housebuilders and gardeners over the years.

His new companion said, "This was a stockade in years gone by, many years gone by. Inside there were wooden buildings were attached to the walls and the animals and men, women and children lived in them. This stone wall would have been a protection against invaders or pirates or enemies. I mean real pirates, not tradesman!"

In Peter's mind he could see the entire scene before it was described to him. He smelled the fires and the animals and saw people milling about and shouting. He felt like a ghost in someone else's time.

"Look out beyond Peter!"

It was astonishing.

He could see the sea! There on the left on the coastline he could see the Priory with its own landing stage and harbour. But what Priory? If it was Tywardreath, he knew it to be partly ruined and largely unoccupied, and yet there it was – intact and smoke rising from chimneys. There was sea at the bottom of the hill on which they stood. That could not be – for the sea now covered the lane on which they had left the trap. "Oh please let the pony be safe!"

"You are only seeing it as it was Peter just as your ancestors saw it. Tell me, what else do you see?"

"Ships, but I don't recognise the ships."

Peter was confused and he suddenly felt weak and helpless. He wobbled and leant against a tree.

"Affecting you a bit is it Peter?"

"I don't know if I am sickening for something. I've done a lot recently, but no more than I would normally do," answered Peter. If the truth were told he felt worried.

"It's only because you are not used to the power running through you at the moment. If you just accept it, you'll soon feel fine."

"Power?"

"When a true Prideaux stands on top of this place, then the power is magnified beyond imagination."

Peter had no idea what William was talking about and sat down on the grass covered stone wall. He closed his eyes and took some deep breaths. He felt giddy at first but that soon passed.

As he breathed deeply he became aware of the smell of the earth. He noticed that someone had lit a bonfire nearby - he could smell the smoke. He also heard men talking and shouting in the distance. They were to have company it seemed. Peter sat for a few minutes before opening his eyes.

The sight before him almost made him stop breathing. It was night time and the fort was ablaze with torches and there was a large fire in the middle of the camp. He saw a tall long wooden building which was filled with men who were eating and drinking.

Some women scurried about the site and in and out of small shed like buildings attached to the large stockade fence.

Peter could no longer see over the wall but as he looked up, he saw that there were men standing at the top of the fencing in a sort of crow's nest. They at least would have a good view of the sea or land dependent upon its current appearance. His current view was loud and smelly and frightening. A man lurched towards him. He was dirty and drunk and was accompanied by a huge hound dog. Peter tried to make himself appear smaller and the man did not notice him. The hound gave him a curious look and then began to bark.

"Come here you stupid dog, there is nothing there," said the drunk man.

Could the man not see him?

Peter got up and walked towards the large building in the centre. It soon became obvious that no one could see him and he quickly stopped questioning that fact.

A giggling woman pushed past him. She smelled of smoke and cooking fat. She also appeared to be drunk.

Peter walked inside the main building and looked around. Men were drinking and there was all manner of meat all over the tables and apples and bread. There was such noise as the men shouted and sang and congratulated each other. A dog came over to him and began licking his hand.

Peter bent down to stroke it and saw that it had turned into a sheep. He was standing in the middle of the empty and ruined stockade in modern 1768 feeling unsteady on his feet and his mind whirling. William came over to him and said,

"You see what I mean?"

"I went back in time didn't I?"

"No, you went back in your memory. Come on, we must go or we shall be late for our meeting. "

William, currently the stronger man, took Peter by the arm and helped him out of the hill fort and back through the wood.

The pony was waiting there as he had been left, quite dry and untroubled.

The Old Manor was situated just at the rear of the forty and William soon realised that the large and complicated job he had been offered was well within his capabilities. The men mounted and steadily returned to Lanlivery, foregoing the planned stop at Luxulyan until Peter felt better.

"I need a couple of extra hands to work with me. Do you know of anyone? Zeb Prowse said that he was interested – is he reliable?"

"He was sacked recently but he does have a family to feed."

"He said that he was sacked because he complained about safety."

"That's not surprising, considering his family were involved in a mine accident. I haven't heard anything bad about him."

"I will ask him later on this evening. At least he will be able to start quickly."

Zeb joined him on his job and Peter got another two assistants, both ex miners who were not as skilled as master carpenters but who were quite willing and capable of working hard.

Peter stayed in Lanlivery in a cottage opposite the smithy at the Crown, eager to leave William and his small bed but not his friendship. He had not been able to find lodgings nearer the job at St Blazey, but the trip was only 20 minutes or so and he enjoyed the journey. By the time December arrived he had finished the job at The Old Manor and got new jobs in Lanlivery, Luxulyan and Penpillick. They wanted him to go to Tywardreath too and he said that he would as soon as he had some time.

Peter was enjoying himself and that was why he never contacted me. My father had discovered his address when he intercepted a letter from Peter to his sister and sent several harshly worded notes about me and the baby which was due at Christmas.

Peter told me years later that he didn't get any letters but I am not inclined to believe him. I doubt he was happy knowing that his friend's fifteen year old daughter was about to give birth to his child and he had managed to reach 35 years old without a similar problem. Ironically it would disgust me to know that similar had happened to my daughter and it would to Peter too.

What was still happening to him however, were the continuous hauntings.

He had taken to going outside at around 2 in the morning on several nights in order to see the lanterns again. He soon discovered that the mysterious event only occurred on a Tuesday morning. It was always the same thing - he would see the line of lanterns moving across the churchyard and come to the lych-gate where they vanished. He asked various locals who made comments such as, "You must be imagining things" William smiled at his antics and Zeb said that he would come out with him to see.

It was Christmas Eve when Peter and Zeb were leaning against the wall which ran around the side of the Crown. They were smoking and drinking whisky while chatting about the work they had been doing and how much money was to be made with the extra jobs. They were firm friends now and Peter relied on Zeb. The assistants changed quite regularly, but that did not matter.

This Christmas Eve was cold and the moon almost full. The sky had been clear up to an hour before but it was beginning to cloud over and there was a threat of snow.

"So we will be starting this job in Luxulyan on the 7th January?" asked Zeb.

"We certainly will and then straight on to Tywardreath. Wait. There they are! Can you see them?"

Zeb peered into the churchyard.

"I can see them Peter. There are one, two three…….six!"

"Six lanterns, yes it's always six lanterns and no men."

"Well this time, let's not wait until they get to the gate," suggested Zeb.

"Right, let's go straight into the churchyard," Peter was braver with a pal.

They ran across the road, tightening coats against the snow which had suddenly begun to fall heavily and fiddled with the wooden gate until it opened. The hinges creaked as it swung, adding to the atmosphere.

The lanterns were moving closer, obviously carried by men – or something which had once been men. Zeb and Peter stood on the path between the lanterns and the gate.

"They will have to come through us now," said Zeb.

"I hope to God they don't," answered Peter.

The lanterns were only a few steps from them and there was silence if you failed to count the heavy stilted breathing from the two men. Peter told me that he had never felt as scared as he did at that moment. The snow falling silently onto the graves highlighted the spookiness.

"I've got a baby due tomorrow," Peter told Zeb, suddenly confessional.

"You said before," answered Zeb.

The lanterns arrived in front of them and silhouetted against the snowy backdrop, shapes became visible. Murky shapes of men dressed for work.

"Who are you?" asked Peter.

The lantern-carrying men moved around until they formed a long line, army style. It was at this point that Peter realised that no footprints were being made in the snow and these men were not mortal.

"You can see them, can't you?" he asked Zeb.

"I recognise them," said Zeb. "Father, that's you isn't it?"

The man did not answer, but Peter felt that the change in Zeb was so palpable that he too must believe that this phantom was Zeb's father.

Zeb reached out to touch the man but it was as though he was suddenly out of reach of Zeb's hand and the phantoms had not moved. They stood in their line - with lanterns aloft, apparently not sure what they should do next.

"That is my father and he and he are my uncles. The other three I know to be the men who died alongside them in the mine accident all those years ago. They left early for their Tuesday shift and did not return home. Their bodies were never found because the accident was so catastrophic that they could not be recovered. It is highly unlikely that they knew what had happened."

"Perhaps you should tell them, a good man needs to know that a problem is not of his making."

Zeb began, "It was the manager's fault, not yours. He told you to blow the wrong wall because he had not properly checked the plans and you blew the dividing wall to the adjoining mine. There had been a flood in that mine and as soon as the wall fell, the water came torrenting through. None of you stood a chance."

"And their families?" interrupted Peter.

"The mine owners gave your families some money and that was it. But we all managed and the village pulled together and there is no need for you to walk to your shifts any more. That part of that mine is closed now."

The lantern men stood in front of them and the snow fell. Peter was shaking and whether from cold or fear it could not be confirmed. This impasse continued until the church bells sounded a peal so loud that they jumped, though not quite out of their skins. The lantern men turned on their heels and began walking towards the lych-gate as various villagers came out of their cottages to see what had happened which necessitated the church bells.

And so it was in this way that the six miners went to their last shift, trudging their way through the village and beyond, in front of their shocked and emotional friends and families.

They were never seen again Peter was reliably informed.

The event did not bring my Peter home however. Letter after letter was sent. My brother was sent and he returned to Ringmore with the message that Peter was earning a deal of money and would return when he had enough to expand his Ringmore business and would visit her then.

It took until the end of April before he did finally return, leaving Zeb running the Lanlivery Prideaux and Prowse Craftsman business and taking half the profits.

Peter would return to supervise some of the bigger jobs but eventually sold the whole business to Zeb, who immediately dropped the Prideaux part of the name. Peter heard years later that Zeb became lazy once Peter was no longer there to push him and eventually lost it all.

My father was more than furious with Peter, but he returned rich and with two businesses and he promised to marry me and so the fact that he had left me a young and unmarried mother was soon forgotten.

Thomas Peter was born in the early hours of 26th December 1768 and was a handsome lad with a powerful pair of lungs. Peter loved him the moment he picked him up. That seemed easier for him now that he was four months old and a little sweetheart. Peter called the baby Teepee, a nickname which stuck. He had no input into the names chosen for his son, not having been present at his arrival, but could not complain about Thomas or Peter.

We married on May 10th at Ringmore and Thomas Peter was baptised straight after. We went to live at the house in which Peter had been brought up and were happy.

We had Peter on 14th November 1770, Jenny on the 31st December 1775 and John on 23rd March 1779. John sadly died in 1784 and I was inconsolable for a time. It was during this recovery that Peter told me all about his Lanlivery adventures.

My Peter sold the business when he decided to retire as our Peter had gone to sea and Teepee had moved to Chudleigh with that awful girl we never got on with. Because of her my Peter did not want to leave him any inheritance, which was a shame. But we never saw him or any of their children and never had a letter from Teepee from the day he left Ringmore. Jenny stayed with us, unmarried and unable to catch a husband.

We bought a house and moved to Modbury when Peter was 70 years old.

On the 17th June 1810, Peter had been with me to Modbury church and said he felt wonderful. We had looked again at the effigy of his ancestor, Sir John Prideaux who rested next to his wife. Peter still had great attachment to his ancestors and had written a book about them. He told me to keep it safe after his death and I promised that I would. That afternoon as I busied myself in the kitchen making the Sunday meal to which we had invited some friends. Peter went into the small orchard we had in the back garden. He shouted that he thought he could see a glow by the trees and walked towards it. Then he shouted to me that he saw lights coming towards him. Peter made his way towards them and I ran out to find my husband dead under the apple tree wearing a huge smile on his face. I saw the lights too and I counted seven lanterns moving away towards the church.

I haven't got over the grief of losing my beloved husband and so wanted to write this epitaph before I join him in the coming months.

Postscript. Mary died in October that same year and was buried at Modbury with her Peter. The property was sold and the whole estate divided between Teepee and his awful wife, Peter the sailor and Jenny the daughter who never married.

THE CHUDLEIGH CHARITY
featuring Thomas Peter Prideaux 1768-1842

"Mother," said Teepee.

"Yes dear."

"What does bastard mean?"

Mary looked at her son in shock.

"Where have you heard that word?"

"Some children said I was one."

"Which children?"

Mary's face was becoming pinched and white. How she had dreaded this day.

"It doesn't mean anything. Just ignore them and if they keep on, tell your father, he will sort them out."

Teepee left the kitchen and Mary put down the dough she was kneading and sat heavily on a chair by the fire. Her head dropped into her hands and she felt completely exhausted. Her life force seemed to drain from her.

She had put out of her mind long ago the thought that this day would come.

Ten years ago, when Mary was only fifteen years old, she became determinedly aware of the 35 year old Peter Prideaux. He was a master carpenter who had a house near to the Wills family home at Aymer Cove, Ringmore. He was a fine, handsome man who had attracted many young women during his life. There had been several dalliances, but no marriages. There were also rumours that several children in the neighbourhood were being brought up by and unsuspecting men who believed their girls when they were told they were pregnant and must therefore marry.

She had got pregnant and given birth to Thomas Peter at Christmas 1768, but it took until May the following year to persuade Peter to marry and have the boy christened. That fact had been a source of gossip for the small minded of Ringmore and now apparently someone had passed on the information to their child.

Mary looked up from her crying as she felt an arm around her shoulder.

"I just found out what happened. I'll sort it," said her husband.

Peter went outside to find his son. He was playing with his horse and so Peter took him down to the cove in order to explain everything in as much detail as he thought Thomas could understand and left him in no doubt how loved he was.

The talk comforted Teepee but he was now niggled by the idea that his father had been forced to love him and that his mother had been taken advantage of by a much older man. The newly discovered knowledge drove a wedge between them that was never really removed.

Thomas nevertheless had a good life at home and learned his trade as a carpenter from his father. Then, when he was twenty four he made friends with an older girl called Charity Strong. She was the daughter of Edwin Strong, a builder from Bishop Steignton and who often worked with Peter. One day he brought her to visit them at Ringmore and Teepee was immediately smitten.

He began to insist that he should now be called Thomas as Charity had said that Teepee was a baby's name. Mary disliked the girl from the first time she met her. Mary was only thirty nine to Charity's twenty nine and looked young for her age. Charity flounced and made negative little asides which women notice where men do not. She was five years older than Thomas and in need of a husband before it was too late.

Charity lodged with her aunt at St Ann's Chapel and acted as her companion. All the better to get near to my son, thought Mary. She dare not say anything, remembering perfectly well how she had laid a trap for her Peter.

"Don't get her with child Teepee," she said.

"Mother! Charity is not like that. She has more respect for herself and her family!"

There was an immediate silence as Thomas suddenly remembered his own start in life and Mary almost cried now that her son had thrown this insult in her face and both knew that it could never be taken back satisfactorily.

"I am so sorry mother. I did not mean to say that. I did not think."

But of course the damage was done.

When Thomas told his parents a few weeks later that Charity was pregnant and so of course he must marry her, Mary folded her arms, pursed her lips and walked away from her son.

Peter said,

"I will try and find you a cottage in the village son and you can stay here once you get married if we haven't found one by then."

"Thanks father but Charity wants to get married from home at her own church and her father has found me some work with a friend of his in Chudleigh."

"You will break your mother's heart," Peter said.

Thomas shrugged his shoulders, "I have to think of my own family now father."

"What about the business son? I've worked all this time for my family and wanted you and Peter to take over from me!"

"That is your dream and not mine. Anyway, Peter wants to go to sea, he's obsessed with it. Your life is not what we want. Ringmore is just too boring for the young - we want to live a bit father. I don't want to be like you, you tried to escape and then came back and bored yourself stupid for the rest of your life."

"I came back for you, you ungrateful boy. We never heard you speak in this way until that Charity Strong turned up. Now she will be happy if you never see us again."

"We want you to come to the wedding."

"I'm not going to your wedding to that woman and I doubt your mother will go without me."

And it was as simple as that. Thomas left home, his parents did not attend the wedding and neither did his brother or sister. Charity said that they were selfish people and Thomas was so smitten with his new wife, that he did not recognise the damage that had been caused until he was much older.

Thomas soon discovered that the Chudleigh work was not quite what had been promised and neither was the cottage. Thomas tentatively proposed to Charity that they return to Ringmore and make peace with his parents. Her hysterical and nasty reaction ensured that he never asked the question again.

After they married and had their son Thomas at Bishop Steignton, they moved to poor lodgings on Fore Street in Chudleigh. Edwin Strong blamed a sudden downturn in work and was very sorry – he said – that he must leave Thomas and Charity to fend for themselves.

The lodgings were disgraceful, with damp and leaks and rats. Thomas had never lived this way in his life although naturally had seen the poorer members of his community in South Devon suffer this way. They were paying sixteen guineas a year to William Burrel, Edwin Strong's friend, who said he had been told that Thomas would do all the work required at the property in order to bring it up to a decent living standard. Thomas constantly reminded his landlord that sixteen guineas was a rent payable on a far superior house and that it was the landlord's responsibility to repair. Burrel told him to find one then but to be aware that he was responsible for the rest of the lease.

One night Thomas put young Thomas to sleep in his crib which was in the corner of their room. There were three upstairs rooms, all of which were designated as bedrooms, but there was only one which overlooked Fore Street that was fit to sleep in.

"Just fix the place up!" nagged Charity.

"Why? It will cost us a fortune to get the place anything like it should be. I'm going to find us a better place instead."

Charity would stamp about the place, letting everyone know how she felt.

This night, Charity was not in the house. She had taken to meeting other ladies of the town every Tuesday where they discussed their businesses and how they could further their interests and social climb via trade. It had not always been like this, there being in the early days a hearing where Thomas had to prove his apprenticeship but also his birth. He was sure that Burrel and Edwin Strong had collaborated in order to – what – shame him? Embarrass him? Get rid of him? It worried him that he could not get to the bottom of it.

In 1794 Thomas Prideaux swore before two Justices of the Peace at Chudleigh that he was a fully qualified carpenter and that although his parents were not married at the time of his birth , they were married during the following May and he was duly baptised. It did mean that everyone who was interested in gossip in Chudleigh and its surrounds knew about his start in life. Charity said that it was a stain on their character and Thomas said nothing following the court hearing. He was allowed to live and work in Chudleigh and that was enough for now.

It did not affect the work he was given, but he knew full well that the name 'Tom the Base' was used in reference to him - behind his back of course.

Thomas sang to his son using a song he remembered his mother singing to him 25 years ago. He felt a tear come to his eye for he had not spoken to any of his family since he had left Ringmore to marry. He wished he could go back and show off this little boy.

The candle flickered in its sconce and the room became suddenly very cold. Thomas snuggled his boy in his blanket and made sure that he was comfortable before he went to check the candle. He lit another one in case this one went out. Little Tom liked a night light and Thomas recalled how scared he had been at night when he was a boy. That old mill at Aymer had made such dreadful creaks and he often saw the white figure of an old man running away at night. His brother said he had seen the ghost a blood soaked woman jump into the pond.

Thomas walked out onto the landing and went to have another look at the two upstairs rooms in case they looked any more habitable. They didn't and he mentally began to tick the work necessary. The room he was in currently overlooked Fore Street as did his own room. He opened the creaking window as far is it would go and looked out. He saw his wife run into the Hall with a couple of her friends and they were laughing and having more fun than she ever appeared to do with him. There was the baker's wife and the watchmaker's wife and the woman from the laundry. Most of the tradeswomen of the town seemed to attend the meetings these days. He pulled the window shut, conscious that spying never brought the spy satisfaction.

Thomas turned back to the door and was surprised to see an old man sitting on the bed. Thomas realised that he did not know who he was.

"Hello sir. Can I help you?"

"Your wife is a nasty piece of work. Do you know that she prevented my granddaughter from joining her stupid band of women?"

"No, no. Who is she?"

The man vanished and Thomas felt his legs wobble.

Thomas continued to have constant run-ins with Burrel who refused to reduce the rent or fix up the house.

Thomas intended to leave the place as soon as he could find any other prominent house with an attached workshop. So far nothing had come available. And they were stuck with what they had.

Charity said that if he left the problem to her, she would sort it out. Thomas said no, he was the man, leave it to him.

"Charity begins at home," she said.

Thomas had seen the old man on several occasions but he always vanished after uttering some kind of warning such as,

"Beware the baker," or, "keep the water barrels full."

Thomas asked Charity one day if she had seen him and she looked at him as though he were mad. Charity and her women now had several meetings a week and she wrote notes and kept files. Thomas looked at the once and was disappointed to see that records were being kept on townspeople, listing their perceived foibles and potential for blackmail.

He even saw his name there mentioning ghosts. The row they had that night when she returned was memorable.

What had increased in intensity around the house and workshop was the sound of scratching and the impression of tiny feet wearing clogs scampering around the house and workshop. Thomas would try and focus his hearing to check where the noises were originating. The children mentioned the noises and he told them that it was the sound of squirrels running across the roof. He promised to leave poison about and remove them and the children slept a little sounder. Charity said that she could not hear anything.

As the new century dawned Thomas began to have more trouble with Burrel and luckily it coincided with the chance of a larger property further along Fore Street which had a bigger workshop and more land. Thomas took the lease and told Burrell that he could not expect the balance of the rolling one year lease which Burrel was insisting upon. As a result Thomas had to present himself in front of two Justices of the Peace for a second time to put forward his case as a defendant.

He explained that Burrell had done no work at the property which was partly unusable thanks to the deterioration. He said he had taken new premises for the health and safety of his family. Thomas added that not only was the property overpriced by two guineas a year, but that the past five months had been particularly intolerable. 16 guineas was the equivalent of a hard working man's yearly income. The property was infested by rats and other vermin which kept his family awake at night. He declared that it was not fit for human inhabitation and asked to be relieved of the contract. William Burrell insisted that it was perfectly reasonable to expect Thomas to pay 16 guineas and do all the necessary repairs to the property. He denied vermin infestation, saying that he had seen no evidence of such. They ruled in Thomas's favour telling him that he could withdraw from the lease so long as he paid for the time he had lived there and all other charges were to be waived.

Burrell was furious and Thomas vowed to make him pay by stealing some of his business. Charity told him that their Honours were particular friends of hers and had helped Thomas win his case.

The new property was only 12 guineas a year with an option to buy after five years residency. The new house suited the Prideaux family well and trade increased and the children went to school and Charity would do her housework and then go to her meetings. She kept her files meticulously up to date and locked them in the cellar where they could not be accessed. It had been suggested that they should be kept somewhere else by her women followers, but Charity refused.

Thomas soon recognised that Charity had an uncanny knack of guessing what was going to happen in the town.

"It is easy to work out," she told him.

The only problem Thomas now experienced was the continuance of the vermin problem. The scampering increased as time went on. During dark nights and ignorant of lamps lit or not, the invaders took charge of their domain. The tap tapping of tiny feet wearing hobnail boots was heard at random and frightened the children. Thomas could not find the nests or the entrance points or even their pathways. He laid traps and poison and caught nothing.

Charity told them that they were all mad.

They had bought their Fore Street property and now Charity had her eye on an out of town farm and land.

"We can't afford that yet Charity," Thomas said.

"We have insurance and if anything were to happen to Fore Street, we would get a tidy sum."

"Like what?" Thomas asked her. He knew that they were paying a ridiculous sum every year against disaster. Charity's ladies had arranged a bulk deal with some new Insurance Society.

"Well there was the Great Fire of London, for an example."

Thomas ignored her then as he did many times.

Chudleigh was a very pretty town with buildings made from stone and wood. The other cottages were made from cob and wore thatched roofs. The houses in the central street had been built higgledy-piggledy as buildings were added on through the years. There were still several fields and orchards sitting between the houses. The houses off the main street and up the lanes which led to and away from the town were particularly pretty to look at. They now knew every person in the town and all would recognise a traveller as such. There were many who either travelled to Cornwall or used the town as a stopping point between Plymouth and Exeter. The war against Napoleon increased the volume of traffic and soldiers wandering through the town and some of them were quite scary as they fell drunkenly from the inns.

But Thomas loved it there and wished his family would come and see it. They had never visited and never seen his children. He wrote a letter each time a baby arrived, but had never received a reply. He never discovered that his family had in fact replied, asking for a truce and Charity had intercepted every letter and destroyed them before he ever saw them.

From early 1807 he saw the old man in too many places. Work, home, the inn, the stable, on walks. Everywhere. He would raise his fingers and point to his eyes and ears. Thomas assumed he meant he should keep them open, but in what regard he knew not. The scampering still happened on a regular basis, but apart from establishing that it must somehow be centred on the cellar, Thomas found nothing. The family were mostly used to the noises and rarely mentioned them.

Charity continued to plan their move to the farm and Thomas continued to remind her that they could not afford it.

"Wait and see," she would answer.

In May 1807 Chudleigh was looking its best. There had been a drought and the roads were dusty. Even the heavy through traffic of coaches and their passengers and the passing tradesmen did not affect the unusual cleanliness of the town.

Thomas and Charity were taking a walk one Thursday evening in May. They were so well established in business and society that they knew almost everyone in Chudleigh. They walked arm in arm down the main street smiling and waving to their neighbours. Determined to enjoy the lovely evening a little longer, they turned down Mill Lane and walked out towards Ugbrooke. They walked over a little bridge and looked at the water for a time.

"Chudleigh is a lovely place," said Charity.

"I love it," answered Thomas.

"It won't be long before we move," she said.

"I don't know how. We haven't any spare money."

"Soon, you see. Then I won't have to worry that someone might kidnap one of my children."

Thomas told her she was ridiculous, although this was one of the few towns in Devon where so many strangers passed through and there could be no mistaking the fact that children were being kidnapped from around the country to satisfy, God knows what desire.

They stopped in front of one cottage where their friend George lived. The couple were out on the front tending the garden which was already ablaze with colour. It was difficult to tell where the plants ended and the thatch began.

"May is the best month," said George. "My vegetables are coming up well and the wife is pleased because she has managed to get everything in the cottage clean and dry!"

Charity understood the last comment. The winter made the place so dirty no matter how hard a woman worked to clean up. It was lovely to have the sun shining in through clean windows onto spotless floors and fresh linen around the house. She breathed in deeply and smiled.

"I do love it here," she repeated.

"You already said!"

They wandered on for another hour leaving the lane and walking across the fields to the woods and spent an hour quietly there. This wood was next to the farm where Charity was adamant they would be living in very soon. It was late when they got back home in the soft dark. The babies were being looked after by a neighbour who had fallen asleep in the kitchen.

Charity gently nudged her and after apologies and a drink, every one made their way to bed. Before he fell asleep, Thomas saw the old man standing shimmering in the corner of their room. He held up his hands to his face and they set on fire. Soon the spirit was ablaze and the room became orange and yellow. Unaffected by the flames were dreadful black and hairy creatures which ran all over the man and made him scream in complaint. They chewed on him and ran up and down his body with their many legs, too many legs. Thomas couldn't decide if they had eight or more.

"No!" he shouted and the noise woke Charity.

"What on earth is the matter with you?" she asked, sitting bolt upright in bed.

The flaming spook and the little spiky creatures had vanished. They were alone in the dark night reflecting only the lights from the houses in the street. There was complete silence.

In the morning after seeing Thomas to work and the children to school, Charity set about cleaning up and moving belongings around. She was excited about today. It felt different.

It was nearly lunchtime before she thought she smelt smoke.

It was almost at the same time that Thomas, working in his workshop at the rear of the property thought the same thing. They met in the yard as they left their respective workstations.

"Something is on fire," Thomas said with great understatement.

"Look, there is smoke over there," Charity said, trying to suppress the panic she was beginning to feel inside. She had seen farm buildings go up in smoke when she was a little girl and the speed of the destruction still scared her. Now this was all too real.

"Pack up your important tools Thomas and move them to the cellar. Quickly!"

This he did and was surprised to see so many boxes already down there. He closed the lid.

"Make sure both doors are closed," insisted Charity.

They ran onto Fore Street and noticed many of their neighbours either running to or away from the smoke and flames which were now becoming obvious. There was a terrifying crackling and fizzing sound carried upon the air.

"What has happened?" asked Thomas of a neighbour who was running towards them.

"The bakery caught fire and now it is spreading, very fast Tom, look after your house and family!"

Charity felt as though she was rooted to the spot - just as she had been as a child. Even on this very hot May morning, she could feel the heat from the distant fire.

Emboldened, she ran back inside and picked up little Peter. The children at school should be safe as they were further away from the fire than the house was. Charity put Peter in the little cart they owned and Thomas got the pony ready to pull it. They both loaded food and clothes on the cart and got ready to move away south of the fire. The flames and heat were galloping towards their home, skipping from one roof to the next. There was a constant cracking sound as fresh thatch and wood caught fire.

The wind was blowing little arrows of lighted thatch further along the street and setting fire to houses which were not directly in the path of the fire. This was a very frightening place to be. They could hear screaming and the crashing of buildings and Thomas just wanted to save his family.

"Please Lord, save my family," he repeated over and over again. He knew there was a family prayer that he should repeat, but he couldn't remember it. He should have listened to his father more carefully.

Just as Thomas was about to say that they should go to the school, they saw John running towards them. He was white faced and looked as though he had been crying.

Charity opened her arms wide and John ran into them and hugged her close. She asked about his brother and sister.

"They are still at school mother," he answered.

She let John go and find his friend and told him to keep away from the fire. John was a loner and quite capable of taking care of himself. He would be quite safe.

Thomas told his wife to get to the cart and start the pony moving away towards the church.

"Pick up the children on the way and go to Ugbrooke. His Lordship will keep you safe." As he said that, their lovely house caught fire and the whole place burnt down to the stones in about two minutes. They both watched it happen. It was horrible. Thomas saw the creatures from the previous night running over the flaming timbers. They were screaming and wailing, seemingly lost. They tried to run away from the flames but were unable. They caught fire one by one and screamed like tortured babies as they turned to black ash.

"What are they?" asked Thomas in horror.

"I think the fire has solved the vermin problem," answered Charity.

Later that night when the family were spending the night under tents provided by the army and eating food provided by surrounding parishes, the villagers knew that it would be a long hard struggle to get Chudleigh back on its feet. Thomas looked over at the town with the smouldering and unfamiliar skyline. A few chimney stacks stood upright, looking black and dead and there were few buildings still standing.

"What a difference a day makes," Thomas said to no one in particular.

The next few days were spent in turmoil. Many came to help from surrounding villages and gifts of food, clothes and bedding. Charity was involved in many conversations with her women and those whose houses remained seemed strangely angry and disappointed. Charity was full of sympathy and suggested that perhaps theirs would be knocked down in the same way the fire-break house demolitions had been made. She convinced them that they would receive their insurance pay-outs too. Of course they never did. Charity and her fellow victims received theirs and the Prideauxs were able to buy the promised farm and still retain ownership of the Fore Street land.

Most were living under army tents for at least two nights before they were able to make a temporary home in the buildings behind where their houses stood. They needed to rebuild as a matter of urgency and were calling on craftsman such as Thomas to help.

A newly formed Relief Committee chaired by Lord Clifford, had responsibility for the rebuilding of the town and the fair distribution of £21,000 amongst those who had lost everything. Building contracts were awarded and Thomas was a beneficiary of these and was able to increase the income of their business which brought in good money and a secure future.

After the turmoil of the fire and the move, Charity forgot to intercept letters. This time he got the letter which announced the death of his parents. He immediately left for Modbury and slipcovered that they had wanted to see him as much as he had. He found it difficult to understand how each letter had failed to reach him. But, he took his inheritance and some of the good pieces of furniture and jewellery. On routing through the desk he discovered a book written by his father and the records left by his mother. He kept it safe from her. He didn't tell her about the inheritance either.

It was only years later that Charity reminded Thomas of the visit she had made to Lord Clifford prior to the announcement of contracts.

"It was highly unlikely that he would give you the work, when we were so new to the town. But you see I had proof against him that I told him I would make public if he did not help us."

"Is that why he let me purchase the farm so cheaply?"

"Of course, my naïve and silly husband. I wanted us to get on and you were quite happy to stay as we were."

"I would have been happy to continue on my father's business. We would have lived comfortably on that income."

"We would have lived in a narrow minded small community where your mother was considered a harlot and your father a child molester."

Thomas stood up quickly and the kitchen chair in which he sitting fell to the floor.

That was the first and only time Thomas ever raised a fist to his wife, but the appearance of their son John caused him to desist and Charity walked away laughing.

"What did mother mean?" John asked his father.

"Your mother is affected by our hardships John. Ignore her. Ignore us both."

Thomas went to the cellar and then over to the metal store which was protected inside and where he knew Charity still kept her records. These had been retrieved from the Fore Street cellar after the fire. Thomas had been surprised to discover when they opened it as soon as the scorched remains had been cleared from street level that every single valuable possession they owned including cash and gold was safely hidden in there. It was almost as if Charity had known they needed protecting.

Charity denied it but often referred to her files as a nest and her women as spiders.

He opened the file cabinet and looked at the files. There were so many that the older collections were completely covered in webs and dust. He reached for them and was horrified when several large – too large - spiders ran over his hand. He shook it furiously recognising the spider as a smaller version of the vermin creatures he had seen years before. The spider fell from his arm and screamed as it did so. Then it jumped back on to the files and cuddled up to them

So that was what was happening here. These terrible creatures were guarding the blackmail material. Thomas could not tolerate that. Suddenly he heard from his wife a shout telling him to come directly up and so he left the cabinet.

It seemed that John and Peter both felt restricted by the small friendly community in Chudleigh and wanted to travel around the country and see how other people lived.

Thomas spoke to his sons over and over again trying to get across to them that it was not necessarily a good thing leaving home and that having people surrounding you who wanted you to succeed was very important. He was thinking of his own youthful escape and how similar the two scenarios were. Perhaps God taught lessons where you don't expect. If it ended the same way he would never see his sons again.

Charity cried often. She had not raised her boys to leave her. She wanted them to live in the town or nearby where she could watch her grandchildren grow.

"I expect that is how my parents felt," he said to Charity bitterly.

The day the boys left, something died in both their parents. Charity was positive she would never see her sons again and waving goodbye to them as they waved from the back of the coach as it lurched up the hill towards Exeter was worse than seeing her house burn to the ground.

They had had two more children since the fire. When Mary was born on Christmas Eve, they were ecstatic and felt blessed with another Christmas baby. It was not so good when baby James was born in June and died in August 1811. Life was still complicated and unsatisfactory, even when you thought you had the upper hand, thought Charity as the cart took away her boys.

The files meant less and less as time went on. People died, relationships and friendships altered and blackmail information did not seem so relevant. They had the farm and the possessions and Charity and Thomas rarely had nice conversations. There were no grandparents and it had all been for nothing.

What had not stopped was the horrible tapping and scurrying sounds in the house, day and night. It was obsessing Thomas.

One day when he was alone at the farm he enlisted the help of some hardy men. The cabinet was taken from the cellar and dragged to the waste ground at the far end of the farm.

It was very heavy and as one of the men pointed out, appeared to be moving and shaking of its own accord. There was a general feeling of anxiety amongst the group as they cleared the area around the cabinet.

The door of the cabinet was opened and a flaming torch thrown in. The noise, reminiscent of the 1807 fire was loud and terrifying. Screams and the sight of fiery large spider vermin caused the other men to run away, but Thomas stayed. He stayed until every last venomous file and every last spider demon was gone.

He knew then that it was all over.

Charity was furious and became lethargic and depressed after the destruction. The files had been her lifeblood.

Charity died suddenly on Tuesday 10th January 1832 following a walk back from town with some shopping. She made it into the house and was found dead by Thomas when he came in for lunch. The doctor said that it was her heart and that nothing could have been done. Thomas was inconsolable. He felt that it was because she had never heard a word from her two sons. He sent up a silent prayer that they come home. No one had any idea where either of them was.

All for nothing.

Thomas carried on quiet with his carpentry business and his children and grandchildren made him as much part of their family lives as was possible. He had a housekeeper called Grace Swales who did for him. She looked after him well and grew very fond of him, but he had no special interest in her. Charity had been the love of his life and he wanted no other, in spite of her trouble causing.

His health became worse during the winter of 1841, following enforced bed rest after a spider bite became infected. On the morning of Tuesday 22nd February 1842 he coughed his last and passed away. Grace laid him out before his family came to see him.

His last words were, "Charity begins at home."

He was buried alongside his wife in the churchyard at Chudleigh.